S0-BXY-630

The Last Night I Spent with You

BY MAYRA MONTERO

The Messenger

In the Palm of Darkness

The Last Night I Spent with You

MAYRA MONTERO

Translated from the Spanish by EDITH GROSSMAN

THE LAST NIGHT I SPENT WITH YOU

A Novel

HarperCollins*Publishers*

HarperCollins books may be purchased for educational, business, or sales promotional use. For information please write: Special Markets Department, HarperCollins Publishers Inc., 10 East 53rd Street, New York, NY 10022.

FIRST EDITION

Designed by Jeanette Olender

Library of Congress Cataloging-in-Publication Data

Montero, Mayra, 1952–
[Ultima noche que pasé contigo. English]
The last night I spent with you : a novel / Mayra Montero ; translated from the Spanish by Edith Grossman.
p. cm.
ISBN 0-06-095290-3
I. Grossman, Edith, 1936– II. Title.

PQ7440.M56 U6813 2000
863'.64--dc21 99-086223

00 01 02 03 04 ❖ RRD 10 9 8 7 6 5 4 3 2 1

CONTENTS

The Last Night I Spent with You

Burbujas de amor*

Bubbles of Love

"She hasn't died." She paused. "She's gotten married—come to think of it, that may be worse."

Celia burst into laughter, her bare breasts trembled, and in a final maternal gesture she put her hand between my legs, found me with her fingers, and gave me a circular caress, free now of all desire, a grateful, gentle caress, like the faithful licking of an animal. Then she wrapped herself around me, as she usually did, and fell asleep. We hadn't slept naked for many years, and at first I was intimidated by the touch of her open, placid sex that clung to my thigh with a soft little sucking sound. A few minutes earlier we had made love as it's made after twenty-five years of marriage, which is to say, as

* The bolero plays a significant role in *The Last Night I Spent with You*. Lyrics are quoted throughout the novel, and all the chapter titles are, in fact, titles of well-known boleros.

if we were packing suitcases. Celia was a little tight. It was our first night on board, we danced a bolero, and she even whispered a phrase more painful to me than any other: "Alone at last." That was when I thought about Elena, thought about the dream I had on her wedding night, and closed my eyes. I held Celia close and she rubbed her belly against mine, encouraged by the dim light and the attitude of the other couples, more or less our age, who were encouraged in turn by seeing us. Then she licked my ear and repeated the phrase. At last we were alone, it was true, after almost twenty-three years of winters and vacations, springs and birthdays, when Elena had been the axis of our lives. Elena growing up, becoming pretty, becoming taller than Celia, much more slender, infinitely more flirtatious. Our daughter Elena.

It was not the first time we had chosen to travel by ship. Our daughter had accompanied us when we sailed the Gulf of Mexico—a short cruise: Tampa, New Orleans, sweet Campeche—and she was almost fifteen when we sailed up the California coast, a splendid trip that brought us to Alaskan waters. But this time it was a much more ambitious cruise, the Caribbean tour we had dreamed about for half a lifetime, with stops at islands nobody else had stopped at. After all, which of our friends, even the best-traveled among them, had ever bathed in the turbulent coves of Marie Galante? Not to mention a brief call at Antigua and the happy conclusion, the culminating moment of the trip, that would take place when we docked at Martinique.

I tried to free my thigh from the leech's caress of Celia's warm crotch. She stirred in her sleep and I feared the worst.

But she didn't wake. I covered her with the sheet and groped for my pack of cigarettes. Bermúdez, who knows about these things—he hasn't been married three times for nothing—warned me before we left: women lose their inhibitions on ships. It has nothing to do with age or how many years they've lived with you, nothing to do with being overweight or having grandchildren. It may have something to do with a hopeless claustrophobia that goes to their heads as soon as the ship raises anchor. Bermúdez himself was the one who got me the maps and suggested sailing dates, since it wasn't a good idea to risk hurricane season. "From June to November," he said, "the Caribbean is a devil." The man has the virtue of being excited by someone else's adventures, the delicacy to endorse them, and most of all, the great advantage of having experienced them himself. That may be why he's such a good friend. One day when Celia stopped in to see me at the office, he spoke to her ironically about the dizzying effect the sea has on couples: "The open sea, naturally, when terra firma's lost from view." Celia smiled; she was too preoccupied with preparations for our daughter's wedding. "Celita," he said, indulging his mania for diminutives, "as soon as you breathe in the scent of shellfish, you'll turn into a lioness." It was another of Bermúdez's theories: warm waters, the sea of the Antilles most of all, smelled of decomposing shellfish. "And decomposing shellfish, as you know, is the scent of woman."

Elena was married in March. The groom chose his own birthday for the wedding. And she happily agreed, and her mother agreed, and I myself agreed, devastated to see her ruin her life by joining forever with that young scoundrel who for more than two years had been butchering her with impunity in the backseat of his car. I used to spy on them in the middle of the night, hiding behind the blinds when he brought her home. First Elena would get out, look all around, and climb back in through the rear door; then he did the same, less cautiously, unzipping his pants before plunging in for the kill. Half an hour later they would reemerge, one on each side of the car, Elena pale as she straightened her skirt, and he more serene, tucking in his shirt, buckling his belt, and yawning. The next morning I would mention it to Celia, who immediately sided with her daughter; in the car they could talk more freely, she said, and besides, in no time they'd be married. The result was that on their wedding night I dreamed I was in Alberto's car—my son-in-law's name is Alberto—and now I was the one butchering a girl, not my daughter but her best friend. I told the dream to Bermúdez as if I were telling a joke, with a sarcastic little laugh, though on the inside I harbored the fear, the nauseating certainty that I was not saying the most important part. "Is she any good?" Bermúdez asked. I looked at him in bewilderment, and he thought I hadn't understood; he rubbed his hands together before he repeated: "I'm asking if your daughter's friend is any good." In the dream, yes; in real life, I really hadn't noticed. I never liked young girls, not even when I was the right age for them. Celia, for example, is three years my senior, and she was one of the youngest women I'd ever been with. When I was eighteen I became involved with a woman born the same year as my mother. And at the age of twenty-five, a few months before my wedding, I was ready to throw it all away for a mulatta who sang *rancheras* and with whom I celebrated my farewell to bachelorhood, and her fifty-second birthday.

My life became stable with Celia, and in all these years I don't recall being unfaithful to her more than two or three times, when she was away visiting her ailing father, which is the most common reason wives leave their husbands alone. Those infidelities left me completely unsatisfied. The next day I'd wake with a kind of hangover of the soul, I'd get up in a terrible mood and couldn't think of the face of my casual companion without retching. After a few weeks Celia would return, holding Elena by the hand and rummaging in every corner of the house as if she expected to find some clue. At the sight of our daughter I would become sick with remorse, embrace her with something resembling despair, and embrace her mother, who would stare at me the whole time, a hard, icy stare, an unbearable look. I never knew if Celia suspected anything about my miserable escapades—for her part she would come home radiant. Her father's grave illness had a rejuvenating effect not only on her face but on her behavior. We would leave Elena playing in the living room, and she would pull me to bed, as horny as an alley cat, and push me facedown, facedown first, and straddle the back of my neck. "Now, turn over." I obeyed, of course, and was totally exposed to the reddish-black universe of her flesh. Then she would begin the Medusa caress that moved from my lips to my forehead, settling for a moment on my nose, just for an instant, then going back, from my forehead to my tongue, back and forth tirelessly, propelling herself with both hands as they clutched at the headboard, rowing intently on the dead calm of my face, a quarter of an hour, maybe longer, until I stopped her by holding on to her waist, struggled to withdraw my drenched face, asked her to get off, a request she tried to ignore until I became more insistent and pushed her back, forced her to retreat, in a fury of passion sat her on her proper throne, unbuttoned her blouse (I never gave her time to take it off herself), and then pulled her forward and pressed her breasts against my mouth and took my revenge on those two nipples that after so many days always seemed a little darker to me. Sometimes I wondered what kind of chimera, revealed when she was with her father, made her come home like that. Especially on the day I found a mark on her chest, very close to her armpit, a classic love bite, somewhat faded because it was obviously a few days old. She looked at it without changing expression and said it must have been from her bra, it was getting too tight. I didn't think about the matter again, but I did learn that a cousin of her father's had spent a few nights there as well, alternating with Celia to sit with the old man in the hospital. Then, when her father was discharged, the cousin returned to the house with them and again they took turns sitting with the old man at night, so much time together in that suffocating room marked by death, ignoring the smells, there are smells that bring people closer than misfortune does. I imagined the two of them keeping watch at the foot of the bed, deliberately running into each other in the halls; I had a clear image of Celia offering a pill to the dying man while that man, "Marianito, Papa's cousin," approached her from the rear, stopped tamely just behind her, gave her the slightest pat, the tiniest brush of the hand, a mere accident of fate when she bent down to pick up a magazine the poor old man had dropped. Celia's guard went up but she instantly rejected the idea, and the cousin took advantage of her passivity, her innocence, to a certain extent, and gradually returned to his old tricks and rubbed his belly against the solid buttocks of my wife, Celia feeling it and feeling bad about it, he was, after all, her father's cousin, a cousin who became more and more solicitous and only waited for her to lean over (she would lean over to wipe the old man's lips) to attack without compassion or deceit, even introducing his weapon under her clothes, panting slightly when he wished them both, father and daughter, good night, it was time for him to get some sleep. Naturally the story didn't stop there. In fact, Marianito was waiting for Celia, waiting until she said good night to Papa, she was going to bed, only not to her bed "but to mine, Celia," whispering in her ear that she had driven him crazy, "you're to blame," tearing off her blouse (on each of her trips Celia lost a couple of good blouses), biting her and pushing her toward the abyss of his door where she still resisted, torn between modesty and passion, clearly whispering no, I said no, until Marianito, tired of so much struggle, caught her hand, moved it to the bulge in his trousers, and sobbed in her ear: "Look what you've done to me." Our little Elena, who always traveled with her mother, would be sound asleep by then, but Celia could not allow the girl to wake up and not find her mother beside her, and so in the small hours of the morning she would leave Marianito's room and go back to hers, trembling from head to foot, not because it was cool at that hour but because, for better or worse, a feeling of clandestine pleasure always overwhelmed her. He asked if they would see each other the following night; silence was her reply, and of course she didn't return. But after two or three days he waylaid her in neutral territory, the kitchen, let's say, and my wife, playing the martyr, allowed herself to be conquered, surrendered totally, melted. The man finally dragged her to his lair, lifted her robe, moved aside her underwear, "Sit here, my love," and offered his face to drive her wild.

I once asked Marianito's age. "If he's very old," I said, "he's in no shape to take care of your father." Her face tensed, and she looked at me out of the corner of her eye: who said Marianito was old? He was five or six years older than her, no more than that; he had lost his wife some time ago, and caring for his cousin made him feel useful. "He's retired," Celia concluded. "Papa's cousin retired early." I thought that all the energy, all the perseverance, all the will of that damn widower were directed toward winning a sordid trophy: the conditional love of Celia, who, after all, disappeared from his life when my father-in-law finally died.

Many years had gone by since that time, Celia never left me alone again, and consequently our passionate reunions came to an end. To some extent she began to live through our daughter—she has always been an excellent mother. We agreed that when Elena married we would take our own trip while she was on her honeymoon, in this way we wouldn't miss her so much, and when we returned from the islands it would be much easier to swallow the bitter pill of her absence. But we couldn't leave right after the wedding. Bermúdez got sick—"I'm so sorry, Fernandito, you know how sorry I am"—and all the firm's accounting fell on me. He came back in June, still weak, and I promised I would wait until September to go on vacation.

This first night on board I had missed Elena a great deal. I was sorry she hadn't come with us, regretted not taking this cruise earlier, when she was still single, so she could enjoy with her parents what she would never enjoy with that imbecile. I said as much to Celia when we had finished, not looking her in the eye because the darkness in the cabin didn't allow that, and she said I shouldn't exaggerate, the girl certainly hadn't died (she paused here), she had gotten married, which might be worse, but we needed space too, look at her (I suspected she was smiling), guess how long it had been since I'd done that . . . and she touched my lips with the tip of her perverse finger, her lascivious finger that smelled of old shellfish, soaked earth, pure sea of the Antilles.

Dear Angela:

close your eyes and make a wish, then open them, look, we're in the Caribbean, you and I and all those birds we can't see but can hear—you can hear birds flying past all night—the skin of your neck is salty, salty, I like the salt-taste of your skin, inside there's dancing, we can hear the music out here, and though you don't want to, and I don't want to, when we reach Martinique I'll buy you a hat, Angela-Josephine, empress of the warm seas, make a wish, a strong wish, even if God is unwilling one day we'll take that ship, we'll go to the Caribbean, we'll stay and live on a lazy black island, I won't give you up for a black woman, dark kisses for you, un baiser noir . . . *and for all eternity my love will follow you,*

Abel

She woke happy. She had the ability to wake up quickly and completely. She was singing. I've never been able to understand how people can sing the moment they're out of bed. But Celia has been like that all her life—while others yawn and rub the sleep out of their eyes, she sings. She has what they call a good ear for music: she picks up tunes easily and learns the words after hearing them only a few times. My wife has an excellent memory. For telephone numbers too. I've called Bermúdez at the same damn number for ten years and I still have to look it up in my address book. Celia, on the other hand, etches them in her brain, she has a kind of computerized file in her head; it takes a few seconds but she always comes up with the right number even if she hasn't called it in months.

"I'd like to be a fish . . ."

And I hear her voice, her song fills the dark swamp in my mind where I always spend time before I'm completely awake. She's singing one of those modern boleros, a song she learned a little while ago—it's halfway between obscene and laughable. It sounds like a joke, but Celia sings louder on the refrain: "And satisfy this mad passion drenched in you, drenched in youuuu. . . ." She pauses to ask if I'm going to get up, from what she can see through the porthole it's a beautiful morning, and she doesn't plan to leave the pool the whole damn day (in private she likes to use two swear words, everything is damn and everything is fucking). I don't reply right away; I'm still not ready for that kind of exertion. But she doesn't wait very long for an answer, she goes on singing, she goes on wanting to be a fish so she can put her nose in my fishbowl and blow bubbles of love everywhere, "drenched in you," she repeats—she's so crude—"oooooh, drenched in you."

What I like, on the other hand, are the old boleros—there's a reason they've always been popular. The other thing I like, Mexican *corridos,* is a shameful aberration, as if I were a man who liked to put on his wife's underwear. I play the records with a feeling of embarrassment that I've had ever since the days when Celia and I were engaged and she asked me not to mention to her girlfriends that on Sunday afternoons we stayed home to listen to Jorge Negrete.

"Are you coming with me, or will you go up later?"

She's wearing her black bathing suit and a white velour robe that comes to her knees. Celia has always had beautiful legs, and she looks younger than she really is. For the moment, she's dealing with our daughter's marriage better than I; women are always better at dealing with loneliness. I say I'll join her later, when I'm fully awake. She smiles and waves good-bye—she knows perfectly well that I despise pools, and she also knows that today I have no choice: we'll be at sea until nightfall.

"Bye, sweetheart, bye-bye."

She closes the door and her perfume floats in the air, a sweetish scent with a hint of peach and a fleeting trace of cinnamon. When I was young I knew a woman who mixed her face powder with ground cinnamon. She said it attracted men, and considering the large number of gentlemen who sought her out, it was probably true. One night I went to see her and she tried to send me away without letting me in because she was expecting another visitor. I lost my head—back then you lost your head—and all I could think to do was rush to her dressing table, take her face powder, and toss it in the air. She burst into tears, scratched my face, and threw me out of the house. But I didn't leave, I stayed on the street waiting for the other man to arrive, a short man who seemed fastidiously, almost fussily dressed, and who had soft, boneless hands that made you want to suck them. He spent a long time inside, and when he finally left I was still there, standing on the corner, meticulously planning my revenge, and I felt jealousy and violent desire when I saw him brush from his jacket and his trouser cuffs all the powder that had clung to his clothes. I waited until he had gone away, then I returned to the scene of the crime and knocked at the door, and she opened it without saying a word. She was still covered with perspiration, she still smelled of that man's sweat, and I began to sniff at her like a dog searching for the scent of another dog on his owner's hands. The face powder was still scattered around the room, in the rumpled bed, heaped in small mounds near the cracks in the door. I forced her to the bed, I raised her skirt and powdered all her black pubic hair; I spread her legs, got more powder, and smeared it inside, spreading an aromatic tapestry that slowly began to blend with her juices, and the other man's. Neither of us had spoken, and I thought that at any moment she'd begin to insult me, but she didn't, all she did was gasp when I took the first mouthful, sob very quietly when she felt the second. I stopped, sat up to look at her face—she had the wildest expression I'd ever seen on any woman—and I immediately lowered my head again. She tasted bitter inside, up close she tasted of crushed shells, and faintly, more and more faintly, she tasted of cinnamon. A short while later she howled, hit the bed with her fists, and then lay perfectly still. I got up on all fours, licking her here and there, sucking whatever bit of flesh came my way. I turned her over, bit the back of her neck, and at the very moment I was penetrating her, I heard the sharp-edged voice of revenge: along with the powder, she said, I had swallowed the other man's come.

I didn't see her again after that. For many years I had an ambiguous relationship with cinnamon: sometimes it disgusted me, at other times I would wake up with an overwhelming desire to taste it. Celia once asked about it. I said I'd had a bad experience with a dessert. I didn't have the nerve to admit that whenever she wore the perfume, what came to mind was the brutal image of myself, a solitary man waiting his turn, standing on a street corner, obsessed by that fraudulent powder silently falling into an abyss.

I looked for her first in the water. Celia barely knew how to swim—she splashed around like a puppy in crisis and couldn't stay afloat for very long. But it fascinated her to be in a place where she could touch bottom, plunge into the water from time to time to smooth back her hair, hold on to a railing and move her legs. Very monotonous, her swim, very predictable. There were so many people in the pool that I stopped and tried to find her, and then I heard her calling my name. She was one flight up, lying on a lounge chair, waving at me and talking to an older woman. I walked to the stairs and passed among couples who still wore the voluptuousness of their first on-board battle. From that height there was a marvelous view—you could easily see half the ship. Celia threw me a kiss and introduced me to her companion. Her name was Julieta, a difficult name if you're over thirty, even more so if you're a mature woman, relatively mature, because she wasn't as old as she had seemed from a distance, she was younger than Celia and probably younger than me. She had a haughty face with a sardonic expression that didn't quite fit its frame of white hair.

"Can you believe it," Celia said to me, "Julieta already has two grandchildren. I was telling her that our Elena just got married and will probably make us grandparents before you know it."

The conversation was threatening to take a direction that turned my stomach. I looked at the ocean, felt an unbearable surge of heat, looked down, and then I glanced at Julieta. Without wanting to, my eyes stopped there, on her heavy thighs, firm as far as I could tell, slightly open so that it was impossible not to notice the birthmark, a dark red stain the size and shape of a butterfly and covered with hairs. For a moment I was lost in the effect it had on me, the exact impression all those details produced in me. It could have been repulsive—the line between repulsion and desire tends to waver a good deal. But this woman's birthmark, an island rising from the most suggestive part of her body, dazzled me suddenly, not at all consciously, in a cerebral flash that was immediately reflected further down in a partial, inexcusable, almost animal erection. I looked up and found myself staring straight into Julieta's eyes. She closed her thighs and turned her face toward Celia, who did not stop spouting commonplaces about the joys of grandchildren.

"You love them more than you do your own children," she concluded, and asked me to rub suntan lotion on her.

She turned over, facedown, and loosened her straps. I covered her with the whitish oil that smelled of coconut. Julieta, in the meantime, watched me. I could feel her eyes staring at my hands, and I tried to make them seem stronger, more diligent, more skilled, more merciless, I mean, more to be feared.

"Wouldn't you like me to put some on you?"

She wore a two-piece bathing suit, and before turning over she undid the top, showing no surprise at my offer. I leaned over her, my back to Celia, placed the mouth of the bottle directly on her skin, and drew a straight line that went from the nape of her neck down to the base of her spine. Then I began to spread the oil, rubbing it in gently, moving down in a circular motion, secretly swerving toward her side. She didn't move, I could barely feel her breathing, and only when I pressed one of her breasts—and in passing ran my fingers across her armpit—did I notice that she was trembling. She raised her bottom, discreetly, and I had the mad idea she was offering it to me. I turned my head and made certain Celia wasn't watching us. Then I moved my hand under her suit, between her buttocks, stretched out a finger and tried to push it in as much as I could, which, given my position, was not very far. She gave a start and said she'd had enough. I waited for her to look at me, but she stayed facedown, rubbing her body against the lounge chair, hiding her head between her arms.

"Thanks," she murmured. "It smells very nice."

I dropped the bottle at Celia's feet and went down to the pool. I'd never done anything like that in my life. Under normal circumstances, I wouldn't even have offered to apply suntan lotion. I had just betrayed myself, me, at my age, with a newly married daughter and a wife who would never believe it even if she saw me in the act. I dove in and swam the length of the pool underwater and didn't come up until I knew I was about to drown. I had lost control, become completely disoriented, probably this was how Alzheimer's started. I dove in again and kept my eyes open. If she hadn't protested when I pawed her, she probably wouldn't say anything to Celia. But that wasn't the point. Perhaps it was the claustrophobia, maybe the birthmark, there was no way to remove that kind of birthmark, I had seen them on arms and cheeks, but never located so shamelessly, between a woman's legs.

That night we docked in San Juan. Julieta went ashore with us; she had just divorced and was traveling alone, two details that won Celia's heart. It was hot and they both wore sundresses, very light and low-cut; they looked like two teenagers. I asked myself how it was possible that so attractive a woman didn't try to hide her gray hair. One of the many mature women I dated in my youth had a similar problem. At the age of thirty-five, she alleged, after suffering a shock, her beautiful chestnut-brown hair turned gray almost overnight. But not only the hair on her head—her pubic hair also turned white, and she began to use dye. I suppose the dye wasn't of very good quality because after making love to her my lower belly was smeared with a reddish goo that smelled of sulfur. I tried to imagine a dark-haired Julieta, dark-haired on top and dark-haired below, and I was involved in that when she caught me staring at her. She didn't look away and casually asked me for a cigarette. Celia insisted on trying the food at a Japanese restaurant that had been recommended on board. A Japanese restaurant in the middle of the Caribbean seemed suspicious, at the very least, but the three of us went there, on foot, as Julieta preferred, because it was close to the docks, and after two days on the high seas we liked the idea of walking for a while on solid ground.

The evening began calmly enough in spite of Celia's constant efforts to reopen the topic of grandchildren. For my part, I devoted myself to encouraging confessions from Julieta, who, by the way, had a captivating profession: she gave private harp lessons in her own house. I imagined her students, feverish, adolescent, hypnotized, deeply hypnotized by the explosive birthmark fluttering between the legs of their teacher.

Celia ordered sushi for everyone, and I asked for the warm sake that went so badly—and so well—with the sultry night. Julieta, deliciously ignorant, declared that it tasted like boiled wine. I filled her little porcelain cup several times, and she emptied it without a word, decorous, refined, wiping her lips after every sip, looking into my eyes, frequently showing the tip of what must have been an implacable tongue. The tray my wife had ordered disconcerted her.

Raw fish, she murmured, had never been her favorite. Then Celia took a delicate roll from the tray, tiny orange eggs surrounded by a dark green ring of dried seaweed, quickly dipped it in the sauce, and passed it to Julieta. She looked at it, still fairly mistrustful, but she finally ate it in two mouthfuls and stated that it was delicious. One of the tiny eggs had slid under her lower lip, stopping at a point halfway between her chin and her mouth, a soft, glistening little egg that produced an indescribable agitation in me. "If you liked the *ikura,*" Celia said with authority, "now you have to try the *uni.*" And she proceeded to serve her a second roll, this time consisting of wrinkled yellow flesh, sea urchin, no doubt, which Julieta consumed very docilely. I filled my own cup and felt sorry for Julieta, subjected to this useless ritual, chewing everything with a certain reluctance, with a certain inevitable repugnance. And I dug in too, not so much for the sake of appetite as for the need I felt to join the worship service. I chose a tuna sushi—the raspberry color of its living tongue decided me—and I ate it plain, not disguising it with sauce, its rawness right on the surface, something violent and sweet that instantly made my palate pucker. Celia was very animated, she wanted to reward me: "The *aoyagi* is for you," and she offered me a lethal-looking mouthful, a pinkish vulva, the crest of the clitoris prominent on its cushion of rice, quivering intensely under a mysterious powder, a reddish-brown condiment that reminded me, absolutely, of ground cinnamon. I looked at Julieta, who looked back with a malicious, irreverent, whorish glance. I took the *aoyagi* between the chopsticks and carried it to my mouth but didn't bite into it right away. I began to lick it slowly, sucking at the erect, fleshy protuberance that tasted of woman's juices. Julieta saw it all in my eyes; she rubbed her bare foot against my ankle, and at that moment I knew I wouldn't be able to stop. I chewed the mollusk correctly, I crushed it with controlled fury, I sipped its juice, and I hadn't finished swallowing when Celia asked me to try the *torigai,* another vulva trimmed especially for my exclusive pleasure, another throbbing clitoris, this time gray and slippery. It was more than anyone could resist. I turned my eyes, as a final refuge, toward Julieta's mouth. I missed the tiny orange sphere that had disappeared by now from her lower lip, and an instant before I came I put the entire sushi in my mouth, bit my teeth into it, and felt it crackle. Without realizing it I had been breathing heavily, and Celia looked at me in alarm, first because I had turned red, she said, and then suddenly very pale—fortunately she attributed it to the sake, too warm for this climate—and asked me to have a sip of the plum wine she had been drinking. Sweet and thick, it produced an immediate sense of well-being. Before we left, I intentionally spilled some water on my trousers. Celia handed me a napkin. I refused, saying it wasn't important, and she shrugged: "Well, in any case, the air will dry it."

On the street we ran into other passengers returning to the ship. I listened to them making plans for the next day, which we would spend in San Juan. Celia held my arm and included me in her projects, and I listened to her with the sudden indifference that is an infallible sign of sudden happiness. When we reached the gangplank I stopped to wait for

Julieta, who was lagging behind. "Lisbon 16," she whispered as she walked past me. "Tomorrow, after breakfast."

In our cabin, as she undressed, Celia began to sing softly. I thought I recognized the words of an old bolero. I was right, it was one of my boleros, and it seemed providential that she would sing it then: "It's sad to recall what might have beeeeen"—I accompanied her in my mind—"you must seize what will never return."

I repeated to myself the number of the other cabin, probably close by, where Julieta at that very moment was undressing too. "Lisbon 16," a pretty name for a room on a ship, a nice combination to designate the refuge where tomorrow morning, after breakfast, I was going to turn into an imaginary mollusk, a hyperactive eel, a passionate, bubble-blowing fish.

Sabor a mí

The Taste of Me

Darling:

once more I converse with you, the night brings a silence that invites me to speak to you, and I wonder if you too are recalling, my dear, the sad dreams of this strange love. . . . Sweetheart, even if life never brings us together, and because it is necessary we are always apart, I swear to you that my soul will be yours alone, yours my thoughts and my life, as my heart is yours always,

Abel

It has a psychological explanation that I've grown tired of reading about, endless articles in medical journals, shocking reports, even an interview that appeared a while ago in *Psychology Today* (one of those gringo magazines Fernando subscribes to), and each time I find another detail that brings me closer and closer to the key: the proximity of death—someone else's death, obviously—intensifies sexual desire in certain individuals. I'm talking about extreme intensity. There are hundreds of documented cases: the dentist who could not attend a wake without being mortified by a violent erection just as he was beginning to give his condolences. He connected it to the scent of lilies, but in fact the situation became even worse if he happened to look at the face of the corpse, for then he simply ejaculated, he came right there in front of the coffin, like a child who can't control his desire to urinate. Another case: a young widow in her forties lost her mother almost immediately after the death of her husband. And in the middle of the funeral, while the priest was murmuring the Dies Irae, she tucked her skirt between her legs and masturbated in front of everyone. From that moment on—this was an acute attack—the mere sight of the obituaries as she leafed through the newspaper brought her directly to a climax. One of the stories that touched me most was about the elderly man, almost eighty-two years old, whose wife lay dying in the hospital. This poor old man, who had been impotent for more than ten years, waited one night until the nurse dozed off, then pulled back sheets and pulled out catheters, threw himself like a beast on the dying woman, and raped her over and over again, causing her death by asphyxiation and, I suppose, by surprise. I'm not going too far afield when I compare what happens to me with what has occurred to these people. It's been fourteen years and seven months since Papa died. A long time, too long, especially if measured out in mornings, because every morning without fail I think about the same thing, it's my first waking image, the fundamental idea that determines the entire day. I open my eyes, look at Fernando's sleeping profile, and close them again in anguish. I see myself in bed, another bed, the one I slept in at my father's house, and I hear someone knocking softly at the door. I respond without letting him in, and Marianito whispers that the old man has had a bad night and he's called the doctor. I tell him I'll be right there and hear his steps moving away; I don't dare turn on the light and so I begin to dress in the dark, making as little noise as possible, listening for the grumbling snores from the bed—sleeping with Agustín Conejo was always a little like sleeping with a dragon.

He wakes as I'm trying to put on my shoes, he asks if it's time for him to go, I say no and then I tell him yes, he'd better. My father's had a bad night and is probably going to die. I turn on the light and see him as I've rarely seen him, lazy and relaxed, disheveled and, to a certain extent, vulnerable. "Don't watch," he mumbles. I imagine he's referring to himself, to his sleeping sex, but he finishes the thought: "Don't watch him die." I continue dressing without answering. He sits up and calls to me from the bed: "Stay here." His tone annoys me, his voice is hoarse and false in the mornings. I repeat that I have to go, my father, my-fa-ther, is dying. He jumps out of bed, shakes his sex two or three times, and spits in my ear: "My friend here is dying too." We struggle next to the door and he pulls off my skirt, rips my blouse, one of my favorite blouses, and the sound it makes as it tears is more persuasive than the best caress; I remove the torn blouse myself and wave it in front of his face: "Now," I tell him, "now you'll have to eat the rags." Marianito knocks again, this time he must have heard something because he whispers Celia, Celia, and leaves without waiting for a reply. I'm far away, far away now, lying in bed again, burying my face in my own crumpled clothes, arching slightly so he can place a pillow under my belly. I think about Papa, for two days now he's been in a coma, his mouth hanging open, the sadistic tubes coming out of his nose, and I hear the foul-smelling voice of my executioner: "Get ready, bitch"; I feel the contact of his hairy torso moving against my back, his gorilla's paw opening the way, Papa chokes, he's choking, and Marianito won't know what to do, the tip of his sex pierces me, Papa turning blue and Marianito paralyzed, a pain like a burning nail in my flesh, I'm dying, he's dying, "there's your dead man, bitch," and not able to cry out, not able to beg him please not to move, each movement is another wound, an unbearable sharp pain, more than enough reason to tell him it's over, Papa's stopped breathing, I won't have to come anymore, not to the hospital, not to the house, "the best is yet to come," I won't be humiliated again because of him, "it's not all the way in yet." Eventually Marianito will be able to move again, and so will I, "I like it like this, bitch," in no time I'll hear his footsteps, Celia, please, open the door, Agustín Conejo's arm will circle my waist, your father, Celia, your father just died, he'll place it under my belly, between my belly and the pillow, "move like this," he'll stretch out his dirty finger, eagerly he'll root between my legs and find me almost at the end, he died quietly, Celia, I'll die too asking them to forgive me, "move faster," asking God, Papa, poor little Elena to forgive me, and Fernando back home, but I like it like this, like this, faster, don't stop, "the best is yet to come," not yet.

I open my eyes and I'm back where I belong. Fourteen years and seven months have gone by, but I still see the vivid image of myself running upstairs, reaching my father's room at the same time as the doctor, finding, both of us finding, a weeping, resentful, rather sardonic Marianito: I regret to inform you there's nothing more to do here. Papa is covered by a sheet and I'm bleeding, I feel something sticky between my buttocks and I know perfectly well it's my own blood. Elena is still asleep in another room, my daughter couldn't be more innocent, her grandfather's death and her mother's sexual fevers can't touch her at this point. The blood runs down my thighs and I squeeze my legs together so that no one will see. Marianito sobs, he looks at me out of the corner of his eye and I suspect he envies me, he knows I'm bleeding, I'm sure he knows the reason why I'm so rigid. He's clever and suspects that I've had pleasure, had pleasure right where he would like to feel it.

After the funeral, Agustín Conejo and I spend a last night together, a few hours to tell him we won't see each other again. I'll sell my father's house, I won't have any excuse to come back, and even if I did, I don't think I would. He scratches his belly obsessively; from time to time he caresses the exhausted serpent you should never trust too much. And in the meantime I try to provoke him, make him feel the anguish of separation, not realizing I'll only succeed in making myself feel it. I sit up to lick his chest and move down to suck his sleeping snake. "Bitch," he says to me, "what's it taste like?" I go on licking and my eyes fill with tears, what else would it taste like but my own buttocks, my open sex, my wounded flesh. "Well, we'll see what you'll do," he spits at me, tears in his eyes. "We'll see if you want to lose this."

She calls herself Julieta. A fascinating name, especially when it belongs to a mature woman. I would have liked a name like that. And yet, ever since she told me what it was, I've had the feeling she was lying. It was something in the way she talked about herself, a certain attitude, a distance she kept creating between herself and her own stories. Perhaps it was only my imagination, but a while ago I wanted to write a story about a woman like her, traveling alone on a ship. I'm not a very good writer, I've written a total of three or four poems in my life, but for this story I thought up a very interesting plot, with a lot of content. This woman, who's about fifty, makes cakes at home for a living, wedding cakes, birthday cakes, baptism cakes. One day she decides she's going to take a vacation; she chooses a ship, a Caribbean cruise, and reserves a first-class stateroom. She's going to spend her life's savings, everything she's managed to set aside during many years of working, but she's sure the investment is worthwhile: as soon as the ship sails away from the coast, she'll become another woman. She'll use a false name, invent another profession (not for anything in the world would she dream of saying she's a baker), and throw caution to the winds and give herself over to a series of affairs with elderly passengers, neat little old men who'll leave their wives gossiping and visit her in the secrecy of dusk. In the middle of her adventures she meets a man her own age who also has a very ordinary job: he sells tickets at a movie theater. Like her, he has spent all his savings in order to board this ship and tell lies. They fall madly in love, with a morbid passion; he obliges her to shave her head—from then on she appears on deck wearing an olive-green turban—and every morning he baptizes her in the name of the father with a stream of his own urine. Some nights, on the mandarin orange of her buttocks, he extinguishes not the ordinary cigarettes used by torturers but authentic Montecristos from Pinar del Río, real Havana cigars that sizzle when they touch her skin. One morning at dawn he engages in an exploit inspired by the nautical environment: he inserts a compass in her vagina, an oiled and polished metal sphere previously warmed in camphorated water. And she too carries her punishments to the extreme, and in a matter of days has moved from the common whip to more refined torments: she saves the bones of the fish served at dinner, removes the thickest barbs, then dips them in hot sauce—"we plant the way with thorns"—and pushes them one after the other into the pale behind of her beloved. Meanwhile, their appearances in public are absolutely normal, they are affectionate at the movies and at poolside, they walk hand in hand down the gangplank to visit the various ports of call and come back loaded down with packages, like an old married couple on their second honeymoon. The only disturbing sign is, perhaps, their sudden loss of weight, and at night, when they meet in the cabin—almost always hers—they both indulge in a macabre joke, drawing bones on their skin so that when they fall into bed they look like two recycled skeletons caught in a hopeless struggle that ends, sooner or later, with the bones dissolving in the sweat of their exploits.

When the cruise is almost over, they too are reaching the nadir of their private pilgrimage to the center of perversion. They look emaciated; they've gone to the extreme of cutting their fingers for the simple pleasure of sucking the blood that flows from the wounds; they go to the bathroom together so they can watch each other defecate, and scrawl on each other's back, with a pencil dipped in shit, brief inscriptions that say it all: "I will die with Cristóbal," or "I will devour your pubis, Valentina."

When it is time to disembark, she falls so ill that an ambulance has to pick her up at the ship. He is exhausted too but is able to walk on his own away from the docks and to the movie theater; he goes back to work that night. They don't exchange addresses or phone numbers. Valentina, who in real life is named Consuelo, spends a week in the hospital, suffering from dehydration, weakness, and night fevers. When she returns home, she finds a long list of cake orders. Wedding cakes and birthday cakes. With two, four, even seven layers. With cream, strawberry, or lemon fillings. For the first few days Cristóbal, whose real name is Eduardo, experiences anxiety and sleepwalking, both resulting from his fear of contracting tetanus caused by scratches from the fish bones.

For this story I had at least two possible endings. In the first, the woman receives an order from a girl who comes to the house to ask for a wedding cake, pays a small deposit, and leaves. The girl has given her a note specifying the color and size of the cake, and the date it should be delivered, but she has forgotten to include her phone number, which is essential for confirming certain details (it wouldn't be the first cake left behind after wedding plans go astray), and since the delivery date is approaching, Consuelo decides to go to the address on the paper. She knocks at the door, the man from the ship opens it, and the two of them turn to stone. Finally she shows him the order. The man, with a lump in his throat, explains that the wedding cake is for his daughter, who is getting married the following Saturday. He doesn't even ask her in, and speaks in whispers as if he doesn't want to be overheard. Her hair is growing back, she no longer uses the olive-green turban, and the small cuts on her hands are scarring over. Her body is recovering but not her soul. She leaves, perplexed, her face burning as if she had a fever, and once she is home she recovers her composure and begins to prepare the cake. She makes it the color and size requested, she is meticulous in the decoration, and on the very top she places the inevitable porcelain bride and groom. Only in one small detail does she break the rules: before delivering the cake, she fills the pastry tube with purple gelatin and writes a message on it that bewilders the small wedding party: "I will die with Cristóbal."

The other possible ending takes place when she happens to go to the movies and finds him in the cashier's booth. It is Wednesday, what they call Ladies' Day. Because she is a woman her ticket is half-price, but Cristóbal charges her the full amount. Once inside, she chooses an out-of-the-way seat, hoping he will come and sit beside her; instead, a young man sits down, spreads his legs—he is touching her with his elbow—and after a few minutes he opens his fly and exposes his penis. Under normal circumstances, that is, before taking that cruise—her life now is divided in two parts, before and after the cruise—she would have moved away. This time, however, she not only stays but wriggles lasciviously in her seat, unbuttons her blouse, licks her lips with her tongue. The man gets the message and places a hand on her knee, then moves it under her skirt and caresses her thighs. She caresses him too, she can barely grasp the outsized stalk he offers her, but she does grasp it and she dominates it, shakes it gently, estimating the degree of his arousal. Suddenly he grabs her by the nape of the neck and forces her down. Consuelo complies, opens her lips, and sucks avidly, puts out her tongue and moves carefully around the glans, goes lower, comes up again, opens her lioness's jaws and lets in that combative head that does not know defeat. Then she applies herself to the task of swallowing it, a slow, painful process, like a boa constrictor that crushes its adversary at the cost of its own asphyxiation. The man moans, twists in his seat, babbles words full of rancor, a blasphemous string of curses and promises, and howls pitifully when he feels himself about to come, but Consuelo does not move, not even when she senses that the lights have been turned on; a hidden current suddenly floods her throat, a rush of hard, nutritive water that she swallows, gasping, her chest ready to burst. When she sits up she discovers that two men are standing in front of them, asking them to leave the theater. She stands and walks in a dignified manner to the door, and stops in front of the ticket booth. Only a pane of glass separates her eyes from the rapt eyes of Cristóbal; she looks like a madwoman and hasn't even wiped away the white thread dripping from her lips, but she smiles, takes out her lipstick, and on the glass she writes: "I will devour your pubis, Valentina."

When I told the idea to Fernando he felt somewhat disappointed at the two endings and began to suggest others to me. In his opinion, the best thing would be for the two protagonists to die on the ship. They could die, he said, like male kangaroo rats, their insides destroyed by fierce coupling; or like Russian antelopes, who forget to eat during their autumn orgies and then drop like flies as soon as winter arrives; or devouring one another like praying mantises, whose cruelty increases the closer they come to the dark vortex of their delirium. I suppose none of the three alternatives pleased me, because I never wrote the story. And didn't think of it again until now, when I met Julieta at the pool and it occurred to me that it might not be her name, that she surely had left her house with her life's savings, abandoning to its fate, in an oven nobody would bother to turn off, the last wedding cake she would ever bake.

In any event, I've noticed that Fernando likes this woman. It's been a long time since I've seen him look at anybody that way; he changes his voice when he talks to her, he pushes out his lower lip and raises his eyebrow like a Mexican movie star, and in case I had any doubt, on the night we left San Juan, when we were in bed, he came out with that suspicious remark. The birthmark that Julieta had between her thighs, had I seen it? It wasn't really a birthmark but a callus caused by the constant friction of the harp. I asked him how he found out, and he said that in the morning, while I was shopping, they had been talking at the pool, the subject of music had come up, and she had mentioned the problems involved in playing an instrument as heavy as the harp. I was about to reproach him, first for not having gone with me to the city, and second for probing into another woman's birthmark. But I stopped myself just in time—he had already leaned over to kiss me there, moving onto all fours, his rigid sex dangling over my face. I closed my eyes and one of my favorite images appeared, the immobile silhouette of a dead man covered by a thin cloth that barely reaches to his ankles. Nothing could excite me as much as that: Fernando taking me with the tip of his tongue while I waited for my mouth to fill with his throbbing so I could fantasize about the useless feet of a dead man. Afterward, when everything was over, I would be ashamed of feeding on those images, but for the moment I couldn't do without them.

When it was finished, Fernando moved back, lay at my side, and murmured that when I put my mind to it, I could suck like an angel. I waited for him to turn out the light before I struck back: Angels, my love, don't do that, get that into your head, what angels do is play the harp.

Angela, please, listen:

she is only a relative, a distant relative of my mother's. She isn't a foreigner, but she has spent a good deal of time away from here. She'll be in the house for only a few months (I promise), the time she needs to finish her book, she's writing a book, a study of animal sexuality, she spends the day watching scorpions fuck, handling dogs' pricks, smelling mares' assholes. You can see that your jealousy is unfounded. A little while ago she told me the story of a female leaf-eating moth that copulates and dies without seeing the world, the male impregnates her while she is still a caterpillar, corrupts her there, in her tender infancy, and after laying her eggs the caterpillar dies without ever spreading her wings, so to speak, without having lived. Unless that's living, Angela, my love, is this living?

Abel

Just before dawn, lightning began to flash. I saw the light, brilliant and then decaying, through the porthole, and I remembered that we should be entering the port of Saint Thomas just about now. I dressed, making no noise, and went up on deck. Charlotte Amalie was already in view, the red roofs on all the houses gleaming, the sea calm and clear as if the storm had not touched it. I sat down on a lounge chair and began to think about the people still sleeping under those roofs. Black men, no doubt, their arms around slow-moving, contented black women delighted by the magnificent tools they offered them. I would have gladly traded places with one of them, I would have been more than happy to exchange the cold American lounge chair for the passionate shelter of an island cot. Wrap myself in a gaudy red-flowered blanket and, in the half-light perfumed by a multitude of things, listen to the distant rumble of thunder and dream that at that very instant, sailing into the mouth of the bay, there was a ship full of passengers, all of them asleep except for one woman who woke before dawn to look at the sea, the sparkling coast, the roofs of the houses. And from the depths of that serene corner, with my cheek resting in the lap of a black man, discover that I wouldn't trade places with her or anybody, wouldn't give up my stained sheets for her tourist's lounge chair, wouldn't want to be anyone except who I was: a happy, fortunate, satisfied black woman, a black woman aglow with the devastating tumult of so many nights without misery.

As I was thinking this it began to drizzle. I felt some relief, and I was very cold, but I decided to stay on deck so I could go on thinking. In the morning I always thought about Agustín Conejo, and after Elena married I sometimes thought about him at night. One thing should not have had anything to do with the other, but there was a time when I often pondered my relationship to that man, viewed it from a different perspective, asked myself questions I didn't even have the courage to answer. Marianito, Papa's cousin, saw it all very clearly from the start: "There's something going on between you two." I denied it, of course, and went on denying it for many months, until early one morning Marianito caught him coming out of my bedroom. He let a couple of days go by and then came to see me, to ask if I wasn't going too far by bringing him into my father's house. I didn't answer him then, or ever, because in fact I was going very far by permitting him what I was permitting, not only to sleep under the same roof with us but the other thing, what we did in the hospital, an act of lunacy I will never stop regretting.

We began by talking about boleros—he resembled Fernando in only one thing: he had a passion for that music. He came into the room carrying Papa's food—that was his job, to distribute meals to the patients—then looked at me out of the corner of his eye and began to sing very softly. His voice was husky, one of those voices that comes in your ear and turns round and round in your head but is never, as I recall, off-key. Sometimes he improvised the words, changed the chorus however he wanted to, invented phrases that he inserted into the original version, very crude phrases with their poison inside.

At first I found Agustín Conejo repellent. I would catch him looking at my legs—Fernando says my legs are my best feature—and then I would position myself to arouse him even more, opening my legs slightly, just a touch, a way of suggesting to him that to get up there he had to cross a stretch of territory he would never conquer no matter how many boleros he had at his disposal. In hospitals time becomes a trap, you fall into it and then have the illusion you're getting out occasionally. To eat, take a bath, buy a magazine. But the days actually become confused and it's never the time it's supposed to be, the time you think it is or would like it to be. Time passes very slowly and people fill it the best they can; in my case, for example, I would make myself feel disgust by imagining him naked, Agustín Conejo as a hairy gorilla, singing the same old song twenty times over ("more, much more, than a thousand years will go by"), smelling of roast chicken and fish soup, the bland pap they feed to cardiac patients. Smelling, in short, of the repulsive meals he distributed in the hospital. When he worked he wore a pair of green rubber gloves and a white cap. Sometimes he put on a mask, but not always. On the days he wore the mask he sang with a different feeling, his voice was warmer, he devoured me with his eyes, he excited me, moved me against my will.

One evening he brought supper earlier than usual. Papa was sleeping, and I told Agustín Conejo not to wake him. Then he asked if I didn't want something, a glass of milk, just one, it would do me good, just look how thin I was getting. I answered that it was none of his concern, but I did say he could give me some juice. I got up to look for a glass, and before I knew it he came up behind me, it all happened very quickly, he blocked my way and pushed me toward the bathroom, licking my ears, crushing my ribs so hard I thought they would break. I felt as if I were suffocating, I gasped for air, and all I took in was his heavy, acidic breath, that and his tongue, which he forced between my teeth. I whispered no, no, no, but Agustín Conejo—at that moment I didn't even know that was his name—went on licking my face, and he opened my blouse and sucked at my breasts and forced me down on my knees. He still hadn't taken off his rubber gloves, and all I could see were his green fingers moving in front of my eyes, pushing between my lips, holding down my tongue, all to show me how dangerous he was and to warn me not to bite him for anything in this world. He held me by the hair and spent some time rubbing his sex against my face, anointing my forehead with the beneficent ooze that dripped over my eyelids, until I, *motu proprio*, felt the impulse to lick. I took hold of his sex gently and kissed it slowly, I sucked it lovingly and let it go, caught it again and felt it thrust to the back of my throat. He was astonished, he moved away abruptly and looked into my eyes. Then he understood he had nothing to fear; when he saw the look in my eyes, he told me later, it was the bold, seductive look of a woman feeling deep pleasure.

That was how we put songs aside and began to live our own private bolero. He would come into the room and make sure Papa was sound asleep, then signal to me to follow him to the bathroom. I barely recognized myself in that submissive, flushed woman who walked behind him, unbuttoning her skirt. A few times, when we were in the bathroom, we heard the nurse come in to change the patient's I.V. The first time we were very frightened; Agustín Conejo stopped, locked the door, and went back to work without making a sound, but that silence was more dangerous, infinitely more thrilling than his panting. I leaned over the sink and let him come in very gently, holding my breath, listening to the shrill voice of the nurse saying hello and asking where I was, the distant voice of my father saying I must be in the bathroom, the close, heartrendingly close voice of Agustín Conejo announcing the debacle, anchoring itself forever in my mind, disintegrating in my ears to be reborn in my throat, a single shout, mine and his, a mutual silent howl as we both came at the same time.

Then it happened: the nurse realized something odd was going on in the bathroom. I had come out buttoning my blouse, and she immediately suspected, she saw it all in my eyes. For the moment she said nothing—Agustín Conejo was still hiding inside—but when she finished adjusting the bags of fluids, she turned and gave me a smile, a forced smile that I think was rather angry. From then on we began to see each other in my father's house. I would put Elena to bed around nine and call the hospital and listen to Marianito's melancholy report. Then I would take a bath, splash on violet water, and wait for Agustín Conejo. Some days I would call Fernando, tell him Papa was better and that I'd be home in a week or two. He'd ask about Elena, and I'd invent something because without wanting to I was losing track of my daughter, I would leave her at the nursery during the day, and at night, when I brought her home, the poor thing was so exhausted it was all I could do to feed her and put her to bed. And so for months all I knew was that Elena nodded with the spoon in her mouth and asked for her teddy bear when she went to sleep. Half an hour later I felt like the worst mother in the world, locked away with Agustín Conejo, clutching my favorite animal, a stubborn, vengeful bear who too often made me bite the dust. Once we didn't meet for almost a year. Papa had stabilized and in all that time I had no excuse for making the trip. When we saw each other again, Agustín Conejo's welcome was impassioned. Nine months and twenty-seven days had gone by, he had counted them, and I surely had forgotten how he tasted; a man's come, I should have known this by now, had a different taste each time. I wasn't convinced, but in any case I assured him I hadn't forgotten and that this time I was ready for anything. Even I didn't know exactly what I meant, but Agustín interpreted it in his own way, and that night he demonstrated it to me.

In nine months and twenty-seven days many things had changed in my father's house as well. Marianito was receiving a visitor at night; he made his confession while he helped me unpack. He asked me to try to understand, to forgive his taking liberties, but so many years of loneliness were driving him mad. We were silent for a few minutes, and then I said that after all, I wasn't one to pass judgment on his life. Then he took my hand, squeezed it in despair, and I suspected he was going to tell me the worst. He was twenty-two, he said, and drove an ambulance at night, and then Marianito paused. His name was Gustavo and he studied nursing during the day. But they called him Tavito, he lowered his eyes—Tavi to his friends.

Negra consentida

Darling Black Girl

Trading places with a black woman, believe it or not, was all I could get out of her. She had been on deck since five that morning and had seen everything: the arrival at Charlotte Amalie, the lightning along the coast, the line of palm trees disappearing behind the curtain of rain. When she came back to our cabin, about nine o'clock or so, she looked like a corpse. Her hair was wet, flat against her skull like an old woman's, and she had a very mournful expression, a look in her eyes I had never seen before, especially at that hour of the morning. I asked her where she had been, and she gave me a sarcastic smile. On a ship there weren't many places to go, were there? I didn't say anything, waiting for her to feel like talking, and in the meantime I went into the bathroom and took a shower, thinking about Julieta. It was still hard for me to believe that beneath all that sweet white hair such twisted thoughts could live. The woman was an enigma; in spite of everything she was also rather shy. A mixture of timidity and boldness, she was embarrassed at my seeing her sex, all covered with white hair, and yet she was in no way ashamed of the filthy things she whispered in my ear. No one had ever spoken to me the way she did, no one had ever used such devastating, terrible words.

When I came out of the bathroom I found Celia exactly where I had left her, dripping water, trembling with cold. I draped a towel around her shoulders and asked her again where she had been. Then she told me that at dawn the lightning woke her and she went up on deck to watch the storm come in. From there she saw the little painted houses of Charlotte Amalie and began to imagine the people who lived in them. And then, just think how strange it was, she had wanted to become a black woman.

I was disconcerted, but I did my best to hide it and suggested she take a warm bath and put on dry clothes. I felt like going into the city, buying a bottle of dark rum and drinking it while I looked at the sea. I felt like seeing Julieta. Celia didn't make a move toward the bathroom, and so I took her by the arm and walked her there slowly, with great tenderness, with a patience not typical of me. It was funny, as we walked I remembered a bolero that Juan Arvizu used to sing, "black girl, black girl of my heart," and I whispered the words in her ear, "darling black girl, who loves you?" I left her under the shower and lay down on the bed. I wondered if perhaps Julieta, there in her cabin, might be wanting the same thing: to become a shameless, scheming, corrupt black woman, a black woman who devoured ardent, insatiable black men. The day before she had wanted to be the one devoured, and as soon as we were in bed she spread her legs, raised her pubis in passion, and asked me to eat her just the way I had eaten that raw fish in the Chinese restaurant. I reminded her that it was Japanese, not Chinese, and she smiled, pinched her nipple and then put her finger in her mouth, and sucked it as she looked into my eyes: it was the same thing, wasn't it? They all had yellow skin and the same privates between their legs. I wanted to slap her, twist her neck with these hands; lust, to be lust, needs an underpinning of cruelty, I learned that when I saw her writhing under her own finger. My vision clouded over, my only point of reference was the birthmark, or what I thought then was a birthmark, and I lunged toward it, hearing her incessant raving, listening to her call for a Chinese, two would be better, two who would nail her, a pair of Oriental slaves who would ram it into her. A whole army of venerable fuckers prepared to chew her raw flesh, Julieta bloody and well licked, a strangled voice in the half-light pleading for them to give it to her, more, more, more, much more.

Celia reappeared, more animated, drying her hair, coughing lightly. I remarked that the rain hadn't been good for her, and she didn't reply. She began to put on her makeup and then she stopped, staring dejectedly into the mirror. Perhaps she saw what I was seeing: in just a few hours she had aged many years. She shook her head and spoke without looking at me: did I know who she had thought about this morning? I said no, how could I. She raised her eyes and looked at me in the mirror: Marianito, did I remember him? I told her the truth: I had never seen him in my life, but she insisted I had, she had introduced us at her father's funeral.

A thread of rage tightened the corners of my mouth: I didn't go to her father's funeral because I had been in bed, didn't she remember, that was the day I passed the kidney stone. She said nothing and returned, disheartened, to her cosmetics. The longer I spent at sea, the more certain I became that Bermúdez, good old Bermúdez, was a true sage. Women on ships lost their inhibitions, and my wife not only was losing hers, she was also going through a difficult time; all nostalgia has its place, and in the nocturnal passions of the cruise the memory of Marianito had flowered, the indecent cousin, brought back to life, had seeped in through the porthole. I tried to think about Julieta again, but I couldn't get the image out of my head of Celia defying the storm, wanting to be a black girl in the dark arms of her Marianito, her exciting black man; now, after so much time, in her imagination he had become the black she longed for. Because of him she had left her bed at first light; because of him she had stayed out in the rain and fallen ill; because of the memory of his erect and ready cock, his dark cock that envied no man's, she had lost all pleasure in this trip that probably would be her last.

In Charlotte Amalie the sun was shining. There was no trace of the early-morning storm, not even puddles, and a dense wind that smelled of fish broth blew through the city. The length of Main Street swarmed with tourists going in and out of the liquor stores, and two or three times I thought I spotted the angelic face of Julieta, a figurehead on the prow of a ship that rose up for a moment, a blank instant, and then disappeared into the crowd. We stopped to have a beer. Celia was sweating profusely, perspiration covered her forehead, and her clothing stuck to her skin. She took the first sip and smiled without wiping the foam from her lips, a brittle, distant, slightly ridiculous smile: "There's something I never told you." I was terrified that she would go on; it wasn't the time or place for confessions, not today, not in the heart of Saint Thomas when we could run into Julieta at any moment. I didn't even know how I ought to react, what I had to say, how I could go on traveling with her in the same cabin after she admitted what she surely was going to admit. "Marianito," she said, "did you know he was gay?"

I don't know if I've mentioned that the light in this part of the Caribbean has a consistency different from all others. It enters people through the pores and then shines from the inside out, it's the only way to explain it, it's like an inner light that betrays everything, reveals everything. I was seeing Celia in that light, her eyes staring into mine, her mouth tense, her lipstick crooked. "He fell in love with an ambulance driver," she continued. "They've been living together for fourteen years. He doesn't drive an ambulance anymore; he's a nurse now." I was sweating too. I felt dizzy, and when I stood to ask for the check I felt a sharp pain in the middle of my chest. A bad business; for many years I've harbored a small, miserable obsession: I don't want to die of a heart attack, I'd rather die of anything else—pancreatic cancer, a brain tumor, a herniated esophagus. But not that damn sharp pain. Sudden death terrifies me. Celia asked if I was all right, I looked so pale, I'd better have a glass of water. She was pale too; we were like two befuddled, helpless old people ready to drop dead on some street in Charlotte Amalie, a strange, crazy place to pack it in.

When I feel sick, really sick, I tend to be docile, so I drank the glass of water and gradually began to feel better. Now I was simply afraid the trouble would return, that I wouldn't even have time to call the ship's doctor, I'd choke on a mass of blood—the worst thing about a heart attack is that you drown in your own blood. For several days the nightmare would torment me, and only Julieta, her intoxicated sex spread open like a butterfly under my nose, her imposing tits like two huge flans moving under my palm, would be able to save me.

Celia insisted on going to the beach. She was very agitated, and I suspected that at any moment she'd talk about Marianito again. But she didn't. On the contrary, she went into the water and splashed her arms wildly, like a dog dragged in against its will, something really pathetic. At one point, when she was putting on suntan lotion, she asked if I'd ever gone to bed with a black woman. I said no but I probably would have liked it. And speaking of confessions, I wasn't going to ask if she had gone to bed with a black man. I knew she hadn't, I simply wanted to know if she still wanted to. She looked at me in astonishment: "With whom?" With the people we were talking about, we were talking about blacks, weren't we? She pushed the hair out of her face and looked straight at me: "Who knows . . . they say they've got really big ones." She went back into the water and I thought about Julieta, always Julieta. I bet she had gone to bed with a black, maybe with several, with all of them at the same time, I ought to remember she was depraved, just yesterday morning she had fantasized about having two perverse Oriental boys, two young men of typical refined cruelty, malignant narrow eyes, macabre fingers, and offering them the sushi of her flesh, a languid, suspect mollusk that drowned in a tempest of its own juices.

That same afternoon, before setting sail for the island of Antigua, the captain announced that there would be dancing starting at ten. An orchestra he had hired in Charlotte Amalie would delight us with their superb repertoire of boleros. Boleros, yes sir, for doing some dirty dancing, polishing my buckle, showing you I can't love more than I do. Boleros for cutting our veins and fucking and all those hot savage things boleros are good for.

Angela of my soul:

thank you for the record and the dedication ("a bolero . . . and if you find a kiss anywhere, it's for you"), once again, they've been the best thing to happen in many days. Of course I found a kiss, more than one, and fantasized about them all night long. I imagine your ears must have been ringing, because that's precisely where the expedition began, a long, dedicated caravan of kisses that did not leave a single millimeter of skin untouched. Finally, after many, many hours, as I was moving my kisses up your back, the lights in my room were turned on and I was brought a cold breakfast that I didn't even touch. After all, I had already drained to the last drop everything I wanted to drink.

Wandering kisses, kisses of fire,

Abel

Amor, qué malo eres

Love, How Evil You Are

Ready for anything, as far as he was concerned, meant something else. Something more immediate, infinitely more concrete. Agustín Conejo was incapable of complicating his soul with interpretations that might not suit him in the long run. If I said I was ready for anything, I had to prove it to him.

He took me to lunch at a fast-food restaurant, beef tacos and nachos with melted cheese. Beer for him and Coca-Cola for me. He had just left the hospital, and that smell was still on his skin, the stink of low-sodium soup and leftover fish, a repulsive odor. And he was looking at me in a strange way, as if he had only just noticed me.

He waited patiently for me to finish eating. He stroked my hand and began to talk to me very quietly: there were two things, two things in life that no one had ever done to him. I thought this was a very serious preamble. I drained my glass, and since there was no Coca-Cola left, I sucked on an ice cube and crushed it between my teeth; I made a very vulgar sound. Agustín Conejo took in a great mouthful of air: those two things, he whispered, were things that had to do with bed, with intimate things that neither one of us would ever forget.

I drained the glass again—there was no ice left, nothing. I thought about everything we had done: our outrageous encounters in the hospital, the voracious, sleepless nights in my father's house, the fucking we did at the least provocation, with the slightest excuse, almost anywhere we found ourselves. We had done everything, what else was there to do? I had the idea it probably involved another woman, my imagination ran wild, maybe he wanted to be with two women at the same time, the two of us drooling over his smoldering cock, licking each other's nipples, sucking each other for his pleasure. Agustín Conejo immediately dispelled that idea. What we were going to do, whatever it was, would be our secret, his and mine alone, a pact signed in blood.

That night he came to the house with a package wrapped in newspaper, which he placed ceremoniously in my hands. I had the mad idea that it was a sandwich, perhaps some fruit stolen from the hospital kitchen. A very ingenuous idea as well, because when I unwrapped it what I found was a robust, well-endowed penis, a reproduction so exquisite, so full of details and little veins, that it looked as if it had just been sliced off in a street fight. When I finally recovered from my surprise, I looked into Agustín Conejo's eyes and paid him a compliment: if there was one thing I didn't need, having him close to me, it was that awful papier-mâché monstrosity. He sat down on the edge of the bed and would not look at me, but he found the courage to explain: "I didn't bring it for you." And then he grabbed my hand, threw me down on the bed and raised my skirt, pressed his face against mine and whispered that he wouldn't get out of this alive. I squeezed my legs together, I was completely pinned down, and when I felt him grow calmer I spoke to him very quietly, in a warm, complaisant tone, as if I were speaking to a child. There were two things nobody had ever done to him, right? And he wanted me to do them that night. One had to do with the reasonable facsimile wrapped in newspaper—was I on the right track?—but the other one, he still hadn't told me what the other one was . . . Agustín Conejo burst out laughing—he had recovered his usual confidence, that constant effrontery with which he colored every gesture, every vulgar word. The other thing, he said, was a little simpler. He took my wrists and raised my arms, he held my thighs with his knees. I felt pain, I felt as if I couldn't get enough air. An easy little job, he added, some simple sucking, pay attention, some-suck-ing. I opened my eyes and turned my head to the side, trying to get away from his breath, that jet of steam that scalded my eyelids. "I've given you plenty of that," I said. He laughed again, and his laugh upset me terribly: "You've never done it in the place where I want it."

Everything had been said, everything still had to be said. Agustín Conejo was in a frenzy, now I'd see what a man was like when his blood was up, now I'd find out what a wild dog was like when he wanted to do his own bitch to death. When

I heard that I felt a second's hesitation, a momentary flash of terror, a suspicion. But I closed my eyes again. "I'm all yours," I said, and I relaxed my legs, and made things easier for him, and obeyed without a word. I was his because of love, unconditionally and forever.

Dearest sweetheart:

there's a little island in the Caribbean, a tiny little island with the sublime, infectious name of Marie Galante. Angela, divine Astarte, answer me quickly: do you want to run away with me?

Abel

Antigua was a strange place that each person interpreted differently. At first Fernando suspected it was a plastic island because the maps they gave us on board highlighted the location of a Kentucky Fried Chicken, and he jumped, a little too frivolously, to his own conclusions. But Antigua wasn't made of plastic or any material that resembled plastic. It was made of warm clay, somnolent mists, a placidity that was close, very close, to depravity. Black men lay in the shade to sell fried food and coconut shells of water. Black women, drowsy and still, fanned themselves heavily, their breasts half exposed and their thighs dripping with perspiration. In Saint Johns, the capital, the children played in open sewers, placing little flags on the longest, thickest, most clearly seaworthy turds. Everyone spoke reluctantly, everyone simmered unreservedly in that languid, decisive broth.

Julieta, who accompanied us on our outing, was leaning on Fernando's arm because the heat, she said, made her dizzy. Since the previous night—I had allowed them a couple of dances—I had noticed how attached she was to my husband. I don't mean that Fernando encouraged any of this, at least not in my presence, but it was so obvious that she needed a man, I saw her so determined to commit any kind of madness, that before the dancing ended I had to invent a headache and drag Fernando back to the cabin. He followed me unwillingly—the music was at its height, the orchestra had played nothing but boleros, and an air of nostalgia floated through the ballroom, as if we were saying good-bye to something though we didn't know exactly what.

The truth is that I would have liked to stay too. At this stage of my life, with a recently married daughter, a frayed marriage that would last forever, and a head totally empty of plans, I should have acknowledged that my entire existence had revolved around the bolero, not one in particular but many of them, dozens of them; and the men who had loved me most, the only two men I had gone to bed with, both had an almost unhealthy passion for the music. It seemed coincidental, but it wasn't. I had to go on this cruise, this orchestra had to be hired in Charlotte Amalie, for me to realize that people come into the world destined to be sustained by intangible things, by odors that recur, a color that always comes back, a music, in my case, that appears and disappears at culminating moments, melodies that come and go in our minds to let us know that one phase is over and the next is about to begin. Fernando always talked about a philosophy of the bolero, a way of seeing the world, of suffering with a certain elegance and renouncing with a kind of dignity; Agustín Conejo couldn't express it like that, but his words said more or less the same thing. The bolero helped him to think, encouraged him to make decisions, obliged him to be who he was. There was a time when it helped me to think too. I'm referring to that period when you reflect on your own body, try to see yourself inside and out, try to determine how others are seeing you. I was very young and already engaged to Fernando, who would visit me at night and bring me chocolates. When he left I would hurry to my room to play a record by Gatica (Lucho was always my favorite). I would undress in the dark and lie down in my bed. Then I began to touch myself. I wasn't masturbating exactly, nothing as clear-cut, as coarse as that. The exact expression was "discovering myself." I felt my breasts, caressed my cheeks, and touched my cheekbones, my jawbone, the rings of my trachea. Then the road divided in two: I placed the index finger of my left hand on the tip of my right nipple and vice versa, the voice of Gatica was like a harmonious lowing telling the clock not to mark the hours, proclaiming that his beach was draped in bitterness, begging, yes, begging me to give him that night and hold back his death. I put one hand over the other and pressed both of them against my sex, I pushed downward as if I were trying to empty it, all in its own time, all in its own natural rhythm that was, naturally, the rhythm of the bolero. Gatica sang with a full mouth, love like ours is a punishment, and I punished myself, I pinched my lips—the ones down below—scratched my thighs, moaned his name, Lucho, Luchito, Luchote, he was in the glory of my intimacy, in the most intimate, most savage part, forgetting to say he loved me, he loved me? The man who didn't love could never say he had ever lived.

Antigua was a strange place, I think I said that already, but I didn't explain what the strangeness consisted of. I suppose it was in its atmosphere, the certainty that everybody had something to hide, the idea that beneath the sweltering inferno lay another world, I don't know, a venomous marsh that deceived the eye but not the spirit. And so Fernando felt sick again, something similar to what had happened to him in the Japanese restaurant in Puerto Rico. He suddenly turned pale, then red, then pale again, the entire process accompanied by vertigo. I suggested he sit in the shade and rest a while. He refused, he only managed to murmur that Admiral Nelson had good reason for describing the island as an infernal pit, a well of indolence, a thorn in the flesh that would drive any man to drink. I assumed it wasn't so bad, that Admiral Nelson had exaggerated or my husband was exaggerating, and then Julieta interrupted to inquire, in a silly little voice, who this Nelson was. Fernando, all sweetness, replied he was "a man who had been here," and I thought that for a harpist this woman was very ignorant, which surely added fuel to my theory that she had come on the cruise to tell us—and herself—a pack of lies.

We started back to the docks, walking along the main street. The ship was anchored offshore—the port wasn't deep enough for a vessel that size—and a launch had to carry us back and forth. Fernando was dragging his feet, and Julieta no longer leaned on his arm but on mine. I took the opportunity to look at her nails, so long and polished it wasn't possible she played the harp. And the callus on her thigh had to be a story too; harpists didn't get calluses anywhere, it had been a ploy to arouse my husband. At that moment, when we were only a step away from the pier, a group of men walked in front of us, pulling a cow. We stopped to look at them and saw them tie the animal to a flamboyán tree and then move away to talk. One of them pulled out a knife, and Julieta threw her arms around me in terror: "They're going to fight." But there was no fight; there was an incomprehensible argument. The man with the knife gesticulated in the air, went back to the cow, slashed her throat, and when the blood spurted out he put his lips to the wound to drink. It was a vision from another world: he writhed in pleasure, thrust his pelvis back and forth, made exaggerated noises with his mouth, magical sucking sounds, while the rest of the blacks stood around him and waited their turn with glistening eyes. There they were again, death and animal passion, the two things that excited me most in life. And I was excited. I squeezed my thighs together and had a demonic impulse to join the group and suck too, let myself be manhandled and massacred at the same time. Fernando was livid; he wiped away sweat with a handkerchief that was dripping wet and gasped words that came out of his mouth wrapped in a kind of vapor: "A slaughterhouse . . . those savages are improvising a slaughterhouse." The cow's front legs had buckled and her head hung to one side—it was a ghastly sight, a mirage of horror in the burning heat. When she collapsed completely, the same man who had cut her climbed on the back of his victim and pretended to ride her. "They're going to rape her," Julieta moaned, "just like the fishermen in Mombasa." Fernando looked at her, looked at me, and blushed. A reference that remote—and especially one that concrete—could come only from *National Geographic*, the magazine he devoured, memorized, and catalogued every month. The amatory customs of those men in Mombasa, made desperate by so many days alone at sea, formed part of the collection of atrocities my husband recounted when we were in bed: the fishermen climbed onto the dying bodies of *dugongs*—sea cows with matronly breasts—and fornicated with them until the poor beasts expired. It was simple anal coitus—Fernando went into precise detail as he caressed my buttocks—with the unusual incentive that the animal, during the act, gave anguished cries that sounded like a woman's sobs. The fact that Julieta knew this anecdote suggested the degree of intimacy in her conversations with Fernando. The story of the fishermen of Mombasa was not something you told to just anyone.

It depressed me to return to the ship. Fernando, after many days, mentioned Elena in passing, I don't know for what reason, and it reminded me of returning home. It hurt me to admit it but I had no desire to return. It was curious:

the cruise was beginning to suffocate me, but the alternative, which should have made me happy, the prospect of being with my daughter again, and my things, and my normal life, left me absolutely cold. I know that happens to people when their vacation is almost over, they become dejected—nobody likes going back to the old routine. But this trip was not almost over, not at all, it had just begun, and what I felt was not dejection but anxiety, an authentic, vulgar attack of anxiety. I didn't recognize myself and told Fernando that the cruise was changing me. He replied that it wasn't the cruise but that island—and he gestured contemptuously toward the coast—that island of Antigua, or "Antiga," as the natives called it, which had disturbed all three of us. He said "all three" and bit his tongue and immediately tried to repair the damage: "Julieta looks tired too." We fell into a long, stormy silence. Dusk was very melancholy. In front of us were the dying embers of an afternoon in which many suspicions had flared, and I thought of the men with the cow and felt like crying. No one else would ever think about them, no one in the world, except in Antigua, would give them a minute of their time. They were mine, as the butchered cadaver of the animal they had sacrificed was mine, great bloody slabs of meat that the first buyers were touching, smelling, measuring with their eyes. "That island is a filthy hole," Fernando murmured, and I didn't try to contradict him.

When I looked at the horizon again, I saw that Antigua had disappeared. All I could see were the looming shapes of the coast mixing gently with the infinite looming shapes of the night.

Woman, divine woman:

yesterday, when I came back from your house, I sat in the dark to think about everything we had done. That's something I do often, I relive each instant with an exactitude that makes me dizzy, I put on a record, I always put on a record when I think about you, and I pour myself a drink. Usually I have your scent on my fingers, and so I smell them, slowly, yesterday especially they smelled intensely of you, I had soaked them in you. The foreigner came in to look for a book and at first she didn't see me, I deliberately made a sound with my glass and she turned and asked if I were ill, I said yes, I was ill, very ill, how had she known. She began to laugh, it was the first time I had seen her happy, a letter from Germany had arrived, she said, a letter that brought very important information, notes from a conference that had just been held in Kiel, and at last, after so much absurd conjecture, it was finally known how bristly animals copulate. . . . As you can imagine, I was turned to stone, I didn't know what to say, I couldn't think of a single intelligent remark, only this idiotic question: "Sea urchins or hedgehogs?" She looked at me with a certain disdain. "I'm speaking of mammals, of course." And then she proceeded to recount the details—they're so clever they touch only their organs, in other words, hedgehogs masturbate one another. By now night had fallen, I could barely see her face, and filtered through her words was the anguished voice of María Luisa Landín, when love goes, what despair, hedgehogs desperate to mate, desperate to fuse bristle with bristle, one doesn't have to know how to lose, one doesn't have to lose anything in this life. I kiss your long, delicious quills,

Abel

⁂

He swore neither of us would ever forget it, I told him again that even so I wouldn't do it, it was disgusting, I'd never done anything like it, not even with Fernando, and he insisted that I leave it to him, he'd make me forget all my misgivings and I shouldn't be a bad girl (it was his favorite phrase), I'd see, I was going to like it, at the moment of truth all I'd think about was how much pleasure he was feeling and how much pleasure I was feeling, in the long run the decision would be mine, he didn't want to force me to do anything, and when I felt I was really losing my shame (because tonight I would lose my shame), I should tell him so very softly, just whisper that I was ready and what I wanted to happen would happen . . . what I wanted to happen, I said, was for him to forget about that perversion, not subject me to that humiliation, I couldn't stand the idea of having to put my face there, having to rub my damn lips against the hairy mouth of that great, black, masculine crack, and he said, "See? Just thinking about it makes you horny," and I said no, maybe curious, what kind of woman would do something like that, what kind of nasty, filthy tongue did you need to have to put it in there, to lick and thrust and move it from one end to the other, to stop off at the testicles (be sure to tease them and suck at them gently) and then go back to the original mission, ferret out that bad seed, that rank, pulsating hole where, for the moment, all his desire was throbbing—"See how you're enjoying it?"—I saw that I was dying, that I put out my tongue and it didn't reach, pushed it as hard as I could and it was only halfway there, flicked it back and forth wildly and all it did was ache, and did the same thing over and over again until I finally managed to penetrate, and inside it was warm and soft, a narrow little cave that tightened when it was caressed, nothing too repulsive, much easier than I had ever imagined, I might even get used to it (he was going to get me used to all those things), I know you can reach a moment of passion when your senses are confused, it doesn't happen to everybody and it doesn't happen with just anybody, but you can become addicted to it, it's like a state of grace, an ecstasy, a fucking drug, you find out then that you can smell with your eyes, taste things by just brushing them with your fingertips, and most important, that it's possible to see and hear with your tongue, a reverse periscope that goes down and sees rivers of blood, rivers of semen, rivers of fear and mud, a battlefield spy sending word that the enemy can't take any more, it's time to end the attack, take revenge with your own hands, make use of the animal wrapped in newspaper, a reproduction so exquisite, so full of little veins and details it looks as if it had just been sliced off in a street fight, a glorious dildo that approaches, for the first time, the great, black, masculine crack, the conquered asshole of Agustín Conejo, a man of his word who even now does not flinch, does not repent, does not retreat when I tell him this is only the beginning, does not become agitated, does not tell me not to go on, because I will go on, he takes it like a man, a man in the full sense of the word, that other bolero, that song coming to mind to tell me that we're there, Agustín Conejo has been honorably dishonored, I tell him it's all the way in and I hear him sigh, I ask him if he likes it and he says he doesn't know, then I tell him that I love him and from the raw back of his throat, penetrated and virile, excited and fucked as he is at that moment, he shouts that he's coming, he's coming, love, and if I'm not a bad girl, if I drink it all up, if I swallow it all up, then he, then he too, then he'll love me too.

Nosotros

The Two of Us

"Listen to me . . ."

I took her chin in my hand, raised her face, obliged her to look at me. She didn't even want to look at me.

"It's cinnamon, do you see? Little cinnamon sticks."

Julieta slapped me and jumped up. What kind of degenerate was I turning into? Just look at my head, my chest, and down there, I had gray hair everywhere, I should accept it once and for all: I was an old man, O-L-D, a respectable man, an accountant, almost a grandfather, how did I have the nerve to wake her and ask for something like that?

"I also came to tell you something."

She received me with disheveled hair, wearing a sheer robe, I'm not sure of the color, blue or pale yellow, what I do know is that in the semidarkness of the cabin it seemed to me she wasn't wearing anything underneath. I caressed the back of her knees and gradually moved up to her buttocks, icy and bare; it was true, she wasn't wearing anything.

"The man who died this morning," I said, venturing a finger, "was younger than we are."

She was liquid inside, she must have been masturbating before I arrived. I moved my finger back and forth and then I stroked her warm, wet pubis. She shrugged, perhaps she shuddered, and moved away to light a cigarette.

"Forty-six," I added. "Younger than you."

Women tend to handle these things better; they turn away from death so quickly it chills my soul. She inhaled a few times and sat down beside me again.

"A calamity," she said with a sigh, "but that doesn't mean our trip has to be ruined."

I, on the other hand, could conceive of only one way to turn away from the chest pain, from everything that smelled of death, everything that sounded like heart attack, a massive heart attack, that awful word. And right now the only way was to make passionate love to Julieta, make love like animals, devouring each other as if we had nothing left to save.

"People abuse their bodies," she went on. "All they do on ships is eat. And fornicate like crazy. All those old people, have you noticed in the morning that they're black and blue with love bites?"

Yes, I had noticed, but I didn't care. Ever since that man collapsed on deck as we were about to disembark in Pointe-à-Pitre, I'd had the feeling that at any moment I would collapse too. Celia, who had joined the group of onlookers curious to see the dead man's face, came back frustrated at not having seen anything—they had covered him with a beach towel—saying that was the problem about traveling with such old people, there was always somebody who suddenly became sick or simply passed away. Later we learned he was younger than we were, a brawny, tanned engineer, an athletic type who never dreamed he would die in these waters, much less be embalmed at a miserable funeral home in the islands.

On that grim note we went ashore at Guadeloupe. Celia looked very nervous—her face was perspiring and from time to time she would stick out the tip of her tongue to lick away the drops of sweat. Her behavior was inconsistent: on the one hand she was withdrawn and avoided talking to us, to me and Julieta, and on the other she was so provocative, her breasts almost bare, her skirt hitched up at the waist to show off her legs, adopting that brazen manner I knew so well in her. But at the same time, and there lay the contradiction, I found her very sexy, very confident in her body, very desirable. We were walking along the narrow little streets of Pointe-à-Pitre, and she, in a distracted way, pinched her nipple, caressed her belly, squeezed her thighs together, unmistakable signs that she was hot. Julieta, for her part, took advantage of the crowd to press against me. She stood in front of me, used any excuse to lean forward, and rubbed her buttocks against my groin, something almost imperceptible, something absolutely maddening. And I pushed against her surreptitiously, tried to arouse her, poked her with the solid head of the waking animal. And so we arrived at the market, began to wander among the stands, and that was when I saw the cinnamon. I saw it and smelled it. Large bunches of cinnamon sticks sold everywhere with little bags of nutmeg, a brutal combination, a mixture that could annihilate my brain. Celia took my arm and said she was leaving. For a moment I was afraid she had found out about my advances on Julieta, but she smiled her usual smile: she was desperate to get into the water. She was like that, sometimes she became obsessed with the sea, especially when it was so close. And in Pointe-à-Pitre there had to be a stretch of beach, a little sand, some clear water where she could cool off. At another time in our lives I would have gone with her, at least I wouldn't have allowed her to go alone. But the pungent smell of black women in the sun, Julieta's damp back, the memory of the dead man—in some hidden corner of destiny the fatal blow was waiting for me too—all of it unsettled me, produced a kind of anguish in me, a sudden need to escape, to drift with the current. I said good-bye to Celia and said I'd see her back on the ship. I had lost sight of Julieta and took the opportunity to stop at one of the stands and buy cinnamon. Cinnamon and nutmeg—I didn't know what I'd use nutmeg for. I continued walking and stopped next to a basket of tamarinds. The woman shouted the price at me. I took only a handful and paid an exorbitant amount for them. I split one of them open and began to worry about Julieta—suppose she had gone, suppose she had left me here alone in this filthy country, in this heat, feeling randy and pale, surely I was turning pale. I walked for a few minutes that seemed like centuries, I quieted my uneasiness by sucking on tamarinds, and most of all I looked for her, tried to spot her white hair, lucky it was so white, I'd find her soon, no need to rush, she couldn't have gone very far. I reached one end of the market, and when I looked up I saw her buying trinkets. I ran, knocking over baskets, bumping into blacks, being cursed at and insulted. She looked at me out of the corner of her eye. "Celia left," I said. She had bought some earrings, and I insisted on buying her a necklace, it was made of shells, and at first she refused, she said it would bring her bad luck. "Not this one," I whispered in her ear, "this one will bring you good luck." While the black woman was making change, I kissed Julieta, I put my hand under her blouse and squeezed her tits. The smell of her sweat was intense. Everybody in Guadeloupe smells of sweat, but not of ordinary sweat, it's something else, it's pure musk, like a lure, something that stupefies you and turns your stomach, something that inexplicably leads you on. More than a simple excursion, that walk was turning into a kind of Chinese torture. From time to time I would catch hold of her, suck at her neck, lick at her face. Then she would breathe heavily and almost faint. I remembered an article I had read some time ago in *National Geographic*, an article about pigs. The male, when he wanted to copulate, would spit and snort into the female's face, and she would be hypnotized by the smell of his saliva. The curious thing was that the smell originated in his testicles, traveled slowly through his blood, saturated his mouth, and at the culminating moment exploded in a premonitory spurt, the savage promise of another, greater spurt. It occurred to me that the same thing was happening now, that from the very bottom of my swollen testicles a foam of passion was frothing up to my mouth, an advance warning of madness, a substance that Julieta could smell, desire, and fear at the same time. We stopped on the street, next to a dilapidated little cart where a black man was hammering nails into shoes. Julieta was amused by the sign the man had hung on the front of the cart: DOCTEUR CLAUDE, RÉPARATION DE CHAUSSURES. Behind the cart was a half-closed door, and behind the door a dark stairway. I looked at Julieta's back, stippled with perspiration. I looked further down, at her Bermuda shorts caught between her buttocks. You're alive today and dead tomorrow, I thought, feeling happy and desperate. I took out a twenty-franc bill and put it in the hands of Docteur Claude, who looked at me in bewilderment. Then I pushed Julieta toward the door, dragged her up the stairs, and began to pull off her clothes. I didn't know if anyone would come down, I guessed that at any moment somebody could come up, but none of that mattered to me. She was panting, she leaned against the grimy wall so that I could penetrate her, and she confessed it was the first time she had done it standing up. Suddenly I stopped, took her face between my hands, I spat at her as I spoke: why didn't she pretend she was playing the harp? "I play the harp sitting down," she sobbed, opening her legs, licking my forehead, my face was at her breasts, my nose in her armpit, my tongue gathering up her beads of sweat, a thick, acidic sweat, the saliva from her mouth wetting my head, an aroma that hypnotized me and that must have come up from her vagina. "Sow," I said. "You're like a sow." She panted even harder, she moaned softly, then louder, and then she gave two or three howls that must have been heard in the street. The place smelled like a pigsty, like sour milk, like urine. I told her I wanted her to urinate in my face, that I wanted to drink her sow's piss, that I wanted to die and I saw myself dead, floating over her body, sailing blissfully over the damn void. I heard noises down below and I looked and saw a black head, an elderly woman climbing the stairs. We couldn't avoid her seeing us, we were still naked, and we couldn't avoid the insult: "*Cochons*," she spat at us, "*chiens cochons.*" Outside, Docteur Claude gave me an ironic look. Another black man, standing next to him, spoke in their argot, and I thought I understood that he was demanding something. I took out another bill and handed it over without looking at him. Julieta began to walk ahead of me, and I saw her reddened shoulders, her back covered with scratches, the red cloth of her shorts caught again between her buttocks. It was unheard of but I wanted her again. It was blunt desire, a deep depravity that did not depend on my body, my body after all was exhausted and my sex was at rest, the hypocritical rest of the warrior.

That night, after Celia fell asleep, I thought for a long time about what had happened. I recalled every detail with that feeling of vague melancholy that comes over you when you recall good dreams. Celia began to snore. There is nothing more devastating than listening, in the silence of the small hours, to the innocent snores of a person whose sleep is blameless. I tossed and turned and began to entertain another plan: to leave and spend the rest of the night with Julieta. Celia was dead to the world, she wouldn't know anything, and if she did happen to wake up, if she did happen to ask, I'd remind her that she hadn't been in the cabin either on the morning we arrived at Saint Thomas. I got up slowly, dressed in the dark, and from the night table I took the handful of cinnamon I had bought the day before. I left without looking back, as sinuous and horny as an alley cat. I tiptoed along the deserted corridors, the only sound the distant rumble of the engines, the distant murmur of the sea. I reached Lisbon 16 and tapped very softly. There was no answer, and after a few moments I tapped on the door again. Then I heard her voice, she asked "Who," all she said was "Who," and I answered, "Let me in," I didn't say it's me, I didn't say it's Fernando. "Let me in, Julieta," and Julieta let me in. She didn't ask what had happened, or what I was doing there at that time of night. She showed surprise only when she saw me take out the cinnamon. I tried to explain that it was an old whim of mine, or an old need, but what I wanted was to play with the sticks of cinnamon, dip them in her sex—the way you dip a biscuit in coffee—and suck them *in situ*. She, who understood everything, understood nothing, she slapped me and knocked the cinnamon to the floor, the little sticks scattered, all their perfume was unleashed, what kind of degenerate was I turning into? I stroked her cheeks, and my voice trembled when I spoke: "Julieta, kiss me on the mouth." I was turning into a candidate for a heart attack, an easy target for a horrible shooting pain and sudden death.

"You're turning into an imbecile," she shouted. "Your heart won't kill you, your disgusting perversions will."

Then she got up and opened the door. I was to leave at once; what had I told Celia to explain my wandering off at this hour? What would I tell her if she caught me now, at three-thirty in the morning, in the cabin of a harpist, a woman with white hair, a mature woman who had come on this cruise to have a good time, to tell a few lies, and to see Marie Galante for herself?

I begged her to let me stay, I wouldn't insist on the cinnamon, I'd be happy just to talk, about the harp, her grandchildren, whatever she wanted. Julieta closed the door and was thoughtful for a moment. She kneeled beside her suitcase and took out a bottle of liquor she had bought that morning in Pointe-à-Pitre; the label mentioned an extract of *bois bandé*, an aphrodisiac, "the last thing you need," she said sarcastically, "and the last thing I need." Then she admitted it would be difficult for us to talk about her grandchildren for the simple reason that she didn't have any. She didn't have children, either. She had been married very young to another musician, a violinist. It had lasted less than a week; that had been her first failure. Later, much later in fact, her great love had come along, one of her students, a man who could already play the trumpet when he came to her house and asked her to teach him the harp.

Julieta took off her sheer robe, tossed it on the bed, and poured me half a glass of the Punch d'Amour au Rhum, the coppery aphrodisiac that we drank in absolute silence. I put a hand on her thigh and asked why she had lied to me. "Not to you," she replied, "to your wife. Celia wanted so much for me to have grandchildren."

The trumpeter, a little younger than she was, played regularly in a bolero orchestra, and looking at me ("the first thing he learned on the harp was 'Contigo en la distancia'"), she sometimes thought of him. He had his lesson on Saturday morning, the first lesson of the day for her, and she would receive him in her robe, the sensuality of the sheets still on her skin. He would be in front of the harp and she would sit beside him: your arm like this, move that leg over here, keep your back straight, your elbow, please, raise your elbow. She would take his hands, stretch out his fingers (the long fingers of a trumpet player), and then have him repeat the exercise, slower, still slower, that's better, relax your hand, that's it, extend your thumb, don't forget to mute that sound, raise your elbow, watch out for that elbow, where did you get the bad habit of lowering it? At first it was innocent. She stood behind him and leaned over to correct his posture and didn't realize her breasts were resting on her student's head. Until one day he turned around with bloodshot eyes, don't be angry, professor, he didn't mean any disrespect, but she was still a young woman—that "still" secretly offended Julieta—and he was a man, a trumpet player who was only flesh and blood, and just look how she made him suffer. She looked at his crotch and saw, in fact, that she had made him suffer. She was livid, stunned, mute with astonishment, and when she finally could speak it was to throw up to him the fact that he was a musician in a bolero orchestra, that was the trouble with learning the trumpet first. She ordered him to leave her house, first warning him that without discipline and sacrifice he would never play the harp. The man let several weeks go by, and on a Monday instead of a Saturday he reappeared. Julieta was having breakfast, and she offered him a cup of coffee. He kept his eyes fixed on the flowered napkin, and suddenly, out of the blue, he confessed that he had found a way not to become excited during his lessons. Julieta decided to take it philosophically, bit into her toast, and asked ironically what he planned to do. He looked into her eyes: "I'll try to come an hour earlier so I can get into bed with you." She thought about throwing him out again, but she thought again, and didn't. From that time on she would wake at dawn every Saturday, tremble under the shower, wait for him just as God had made her, sitting in front of the harp, playing "Lolita la danseuse," a piece by Tournier that should be played exactly this way, naked and hungering for a cock. When the final note sounded, he would approach silently and move the harp away, but she pretended not to notice, she remained seated with her back straight, her eyes half closed, her arms in the correct position, waiting in vain for him to return the instrument to her. Instead she felt his tongue, first the tip of that warm probe came in and then, with all their strength, his muscular lips began their work. The woman who hasn't been loved by a trumpet player, Julieta declared, will never know what good sucking is. Twice she lost consciousness, twice she felt as if that mouth were sucking her blood, in any case she would wake up on the sofa with a deep burning in her groin, listening to the still awkward cadences of the melody, with you in the distance, my love, I am . . . I was . . . I was there, I made an effort to see and I saw him, saw the rigid silhouette of the harp and the dark shining hair of her pupil—why was it that all trumpet players used brilliantine?—his Arabic profile and hairy arms visible through the strings, and she would sit up, find the little voice she still had, and begin to teach the lesson. He listened to her, naked and attentive, until Julieta said it was enough for today, he should learn La Gavotte by Grandjany and forget about boleros. He embraced her from behind and renewed his promise: "I'll give you a gavotte." He was vulgar, there was no denying it, vulgar as only a trumpet player in a bolero orchestra can be. But at the same time he had an Oriental sensibility about certain things. About eating, for example—he always did it silently, in an orderly and circumspect way, sucking at the little bones until they were smooth and shiny, with gestures that Julieta had seen only in a few Chinese. And his attitude toward light—he didn't like bright illumination, he had her constantly lower the blinds and forced her to give the lesson in a half-light. And they had gone on this way for fifteen years, seven months, and twenty-two days.

"A life," I said, for the sake of saying something. Julieta poured me and herself another glass of the Punch d'Amour au Rhum. I looked through the porthole and saw that it was growing light. I wasn't very interested in the rest of the story, but I felt obliged to ask the question.

"He died in an accident," she replied. "That's why I'm here."

I looked for the connection between one thing and the other. She had come on this ship because he was dead; otherwise she would have remained in her shadowy house, teaching him how to ruin another bolero.

"I came to see the place where he died."

I was startled, of course, but I tried not to show it. I began to kiss her thighs, and she, curiously enough, started to scratch my head. She was very roundabout, she used a lot of clichés—nobody knew about anyone else's life, each of us carries our own funeral inside us, life was a lottery, a lottery, a lottery. I, in the meantime, had reached her sex and deliberately spilled a few drops of liquor on her white hairs, I sucked at them docilely, in an orderly, circumspect way, wanting to leave the little bones clean, I too had my Oriental sensibility. She didn't move, but she trembled before she spoke.

"He fell into the maw of the Great Abyss. He died on Marie Galante."

It was too much for my sleepless brain. I'd think about it tomorrow. Fernando Scarlett O'Hara, I'll never be horny again, and then I remembered that tomorrow was already today, and that today, on precisely this day, the ship would be bringing us to that devilish privateers' island, that beautiful no-man's-land. The island of Marie Galante.

"You have to leave," Julieta stammered.

I paid no attention to her. The sun was up, and I had nothing left to lose. I poured the rest of my liquor on her sex, I had a good amount left, and I placed my hands under her buttocks to bring her up to my mouth. I kissed her there, no licking, no sucking, just simple, sonorous, chaste kisses. I felt her moving her closed fist between my face and her groin. I raised my head, I didn't understand.

"Here they are," she said.

She loosened her fingers and dropped five or six cinnamon sticks. Two of them caught on her damp pubic hair, the rest rolled onto the sheets.

"Here they are," she repeated. "Now fuck my brains out."

Vereda tropical

Tropical Path

The beach was in Gosier. If I caught the bus over there—the girl pointed to the other side of the street—it wouldn't take me more than twenty or twenty-five minutes to get to the public swimming area. I did as she said. I felt obedient and liberated. Obedient to my own desires, to what I wanted to do, and liberated because Fernando and Julieta had stayed behind, simmering in the indecent broth of their constant touching, drowning in their own drooling glances, their words with hidden meanings, that whole disgusting affair. The bus was crowded with passengers, and I looked out the window. I liked the wind, the smells, I liked Guadeloupe tremendously. Even the name Gosier filled me with happiness. I had no concrete plans and no particular illusions: I simply wanted to get into the ocean, swallow salt water, furtively lick my arm. When I come out of the ocean I like to lick the skin of my arm, I love the taste of flesh just out of the sea, so clean, so pungent.

Half an hour later the driver turned around, caught my eye, and pointed to the front door: "Get out here, this is Gosier." I felt a stupid emotion: what did I care if I was in Gosier, or Pointe-à-Pitre, or Capesterre, or Petit Bourg? It was all foreign to me, what difference could it possibly make? But no, I was delighted with Gosier, I laughed to myself, I felt fortunate to be walking along those streets that were flogged by a brutal sun. I asked a fruit vendor how to get to the beach, and he told me to go straight until I passed the church, turn right, and not to stop until I saw the sea. I bought a handful of tamarinds and thanked him for the information. I liked the acid taste of the flesh, it excited me to dip it in the seawater and suck it, with that salty flavor. I used to do it all the time when I was a girl.

The beach was small, with a crystal-clear ocean where you could see your feet, and a gentle surf that caressed you. There were a few tourists sunbathing, and five or six black heads could be seen in the distance, swimming in deep water. I walked to the edge, wet my fingers, and crossed myself—I always crossed myself before I went in the water. I was wearing my bathing suit under my clothes but I preferred to suffer, postpone my swim for a moment, heighten the desire in a perverse way. I began to walk along the sand and broke open the first tamarind, the soft little head appeared and I brought it to my lips. I picked up a few shells, caught a crab, I think I felt a little like a savage, and finally I stopped near some rocks at the very end of the little beach. Then I saw it. A picture-postcard island, a painted Caribbean island, a solitary tropical island. There in front of me, across from Gosier, a little paradise with its strip of white sand and its perfect stand of coconut palms. I stood there for a while, enthralled. It occurred to me that perhaps I was the only one who saw it, that it was a sea mirage. I couldn't understand why anyone would swim on this side and not try to get across to the other. I turned and left the beach. I walked faster, I even thought I was running. I returned to the drowsy streets—few people in Gosier were out walking at that time of day. I went into a gift shop and pretended to look at some necklaces. I thought briefly of Elena, perhaps I ought to buy her something, a pair of earrings, a bracelet, something to let her know her mother was thinking of her. The saleswoman approached, full of suggestions. I pretended I couldn't choose between a ring and a pin, I acted as if I were examining them, in reality I didn't see them, and suddenly I looked up and asked her about the island, the one you could see from the beach, could she tell me how to get there. She smiled, nodded without really understanding me—or she pretended not to understand me—and tried to show me another ring. I stopped her by saying she shouldn't look for anything else, I'd take the pin but first I wanted to know how I could get to the other side. "Ahhhh," she exclaimed, "Ilet du Gosier." She wrapped the pin and extended her hand, trying to take the bill I held out and pulled back in a matter of seconds. Then she told me: to get to the other side I had to pay five francs to one of the boatmen who made the crossing. The boats were down there, I should follow the beach road and before I reached the swimming area turn left, look for a bar called Victor Hugues, it was the boatmen's bar, that's where they gathered and the boats left from there. I paid her and walked out, feeling uneasy. I wasn't as happy as I'd been when I got off the bus. The morning was rushing past me and I had a single fixed idea: I wanted to sit on the white path on the island and look toward the beach at Gosier. Maybe I'd see that other woman on the rocks, a pale, disoriented blonde, we would look at each other, she wanting to be on the other side, wanting to be the woman I was, devouring me with her eyes, and I wanting to be only what I could be: a vision at the edge of the mirage, an apparition within another apparition.

There was a long line of passengers. They were people from Gosier going to spend the day on Ilet du Gosier. They carried pots of stew, children with blankets, bottles of liquor; they traveled with pillows, with stools and radios, with hammocks and bunches of plantains, with live—almost live—chickens. I smelled the odor of dried blood and my skin crawled: I thought about the passenger who had died that morning, we were ready to disembark when he collapsed and died, without a complaint, without realizing what was happening. It was a stroke of luck to die like that. I walked to the end of the line and resigned myself to the thought that I'd have to wait a long time before I could board one of the boats. The light, the fiercest sun I had ever seen, forced me to squint, and I didn't even see the man who approached and took me by the arm and pulled me toward the shore. I resisted halfheartedly, I was repulsed by the touch of that large, wet hand, and when we stopped at the water I was finally able to see his face. He wasn't black, he was more than that; under the quicklime brilliance of the midday sunlight—and the light on these islands never lies—his skin looked almost purple. His chest was bare, he spoke an argot, and all I could make out was that I had to pay ten francs for the trip. I agreed immediately, and it cost five more francs to move ahead in line, but I didn't care, I would have given twenty, I would have given what I didn't even have just to get to the other side. I walked into the water, following the other passengers—there was no other way to get into the boat. The men held the pots in the air, the women carried the children, and I walked slowly, the water up to my waist and my head filled with premonitions. The boat I was going to board, packed with families, could very well capsize and sink. I estimated that there were more than twenty of us, not to mention their food and the weight of the gear they had brought for their outing. I was petrified as I looked at the overcrowded launch, but the people on it urged me to climb in, they held out their callused hands to me, black hands willing to lift me up, I relaxed my muscles and extended my arms, I closed my eyes expecting to be hoisted up, but there was no need, at that moment I was pushed from below and deposited on deck like another piece of gear. I looked at the dripping head of the man who had lifted me. It was the owner of the boat, the same man who had charged me five extra francs for the courtesy of finding me a space, a foul hole, an unfortunate spot in that wretched ferry. He climbed in too, wiped his face with a grimy towel, and took his place at the wheel. I observed him more carefully; he looked at nothing and no one, he pretended to look at the horizon, the greenish-white line of the island, but he didn't see that either. He had slanted, perverse eyes, he was a Chinese black with a diabolical face, a tense, hard body, pure nerve and pure muscle, black, jet black. A chill ran up my spine: I was sure we were going to sink. I started to tremble, I was very dizzy and I lowered my head, it's what you do to control nausea. The other passengers, crowded all around me, didn't even blink an eye. But the owner did, the owner was looking at me when I raised my head, and kept looking at me for some time. I wanted to tell him I was feeling better, but the sound of the wind, the chatter of the women, the surge of the sea didn't let me. Then I noticed we were slowing down. I turned my head and saw that we had reached the Ilet du Gosier. The crossing had taken no time at all, we hadn't sunk, we hadn't died in the attempt. In front of us was a small dock, but the boat anchored some distance from shore, the people began to jump into the water, and when I attempted to follow, the owner signaled for me to wait. It took him some time to collect money from the other passengers, and then he came toward me, turned his back, and told me to sit on his shoulders. I did, I sat astride him, and between my legs I felt the fiendish heat from the back of his neck, I felt the pressure of his hands, his huge wet hands like two grappling irons on my knees. It seemed to me he was walking slowly, taking longer than he needed to carry me to shore. I wanted to tell him he could let me go, I wanted to order him to leave me alone, and then the reverse happened, the worst thing that could have happened, I thought about the man who had died that morning, the image of his face came to mind, his half-closed eyes, a thin white line, blurred, tearful . . . the dead tend to weep after they're dead. I've already said that those thoughts excite me, make my blood hot, there are those articles in *Psychology Today*, my case is not unique, and so I tightened my legs, the boatman stopped and squatted so I could get down, and before I did I moved twice, twice I rubbed my sex against the barbed wire of his hair. Then we walked together on the sand. He realized I had no plan, he spoke some more argot and I caught a few words, another beach, he said, and I nodded, licking my lips. I followed him by instinct. We walked into the forest, which was occupied by families boiling water and plucking chickens. The air smelled of charcoal and boiled plantains, my breasts were sweating, mosquitoes hounded me, the heat was awful, dense smoke made me cough, there was a prickling stillness of predatory beasts lying in wait. Gradually the forest emptied of people, it became a turbid, oppressive mangrove swamp, and just when I thought I was going to faint we came out into a clearing. From there we could see the tiny, rocky beach that smelled of decomposing shellfish. He turned and ordered me into the water: I'm obedient, a woman as submissive as a child. I took off my clothes and was ashamed of my bathing suit, I felt old, I went in quickly so he wouldn't see me, not crossing myself this time, and he followed me in, passed me, and swam out to deep water. I felt terribly agitated. I thought of Elena, I thought of Fernando, I thought in passing of that woman, Julieta. They all seemed very distant, as if they all were dead. Or as if I were dead. He started back, he swam toward me, and I saw his slanted eyes commanding the surface of the water. I smiled at him, churning with desire. He went under, put his hands on my thighs, his hands seemed so big and now, in the water, they became enormous, the huge hands of the owner of the boat, a forbidden black, a sea monster. He spread my legs and put his fingers in me, he squeezed my buttocks under my bathing suit, I said no, no, I made a feeble attempt to get out of the water. Then he put his arm around my waist and lifted out my breasts, they floated like jellyfish, he took them in his hands and sucked them the way I sucked tamarinds, with the salty taste of seawater on them. This boatman had a large mouth, lips as thick as steaks, a tongue I suddenly wanted to bite and that I searched for in the tumult of the waves. He picked me up in a fury of passion and walked to shore, I closed my eyes, licked his face, searched for that powerful tongue again, but he denied it to me. He crossed the beach and went into the mangroves, lay me on the ground, and stripped me in one swoop of his hand, as if he were skinning a rabbit, a flayed rabbit that is still alive and writhing, that was my body, twitching with desire in a swamp. Then he moved to one side, I opened my eyes and saw that he was undressing too, I saw him from the back, his round, gleaming buttocks, two black sweating buttocks that I swore I would lick, bite, riddle with bite marks, and then he turned around, took a few steps toward me, and showed it to me. If I lived a hundred years after seeing that, a hundred years would not have been enough time for me to recover. I wanted to scream, and all that came out was a wail, a pathetic sound, like the death rattle of a cat. He laughed out loud, walked over my body with his legs spread wide, squatted in front of my face, and let the head of his cock, solid and huge, anoint my forehead. I don't know about measurements, I never could estimate the length or width or thickness of anything, but I held it in my hands and was as moved as if it were a newborn infant, it was a heavy, lustrous black shaft, an animal of love I didn't deserve. I opened my mouth and he stroked my hair, I sucked like a little girl, decorously, modestly, feeling at times as if I were choking, choking, the two of us sweating, the two of us stinking, his smell drove me wild, the fermented sweat of his groin, the lethal sweat of his armpits, the thick sweat beading on his chest, his hairy chest, wiry, tightly curled hairs that would surely scratch a woman's skin. Suddenly he moved down, the same hands he had tempted me with, still wet, still abusive, spread my legs apart. I saw his slanted eyes and that was the last thing I saw. My scream flew over the mangrove swamp and flew over the useful fires along the shore, it passed over the chickens with wrung necks, over the heads of sleeping children, over the pots of stew and over the sea that separated us from Gosier, it reached the swimming area and startled the woman still waiting on the rocks, a blonde who nourished the hope of fornicating with a boatman, a boar capable of screwing her with his corkscrew member, something that only a boar can do. The man bent my legs and my bones cracked, I felt a sharp pain in my groin, he drilled into my womb, and I remembered one of Fernando's stories, it wasn't the proper time, I know that, but you can never choose your memories, the story was about some mites that live in the down of owls, the curved claws of the male owls are out of control during coitus, they leave the soft backs of their mates permanently bent. That's how I would be, I thought, bent over for life, crippled with passion, gratefully licking the soles of the feet of that boatman who never stopped.

We returned to the boat together, walking with our arms around each other past the families nodding with drowsiness, observing us with indifference. We went back to Gosier alone, alone in the boat where we squandered our final embraces. We got out at the bar called Victor Hugues. I was bleeding like a virgin—somehow that long tool had reached where no one had reached before. We drank the red *aguardiente* they drink in that place, and I had a feeling this would be the most important afternoon of my life. He didn't even look at me, he looked at his boat, I sensed that at any moment he would leave, and I remembered that I had to take the next bus to Pointe-à-Pitre. I said good-bye, kissing him on the mouth, the implacable steak of those lips, a tongue he no longer denied me, teeth that remained in my flesh so I would remember his taste that night, remember it the next night, remember it now and at the hour of my death and for all the nights I would live without him.

Soul of vanity:

there I was, thinking about you; there were your smells, here your kisses, here and here. Everything was very dark, you know my fondness for the dark, I like to think about you in the dark. I was listening to that song, "Bésame mucho," and I heard the foreigner's footsteps stopping behind me. She was holding a glass in her hand—I knew from the clink of the ice cubes—and she had the nerve to interrupt me. "Do you know that the flea that lives on the rabbit has no desire to copulate until the rabbit copulates?" What could I do, tell me, strangle her, slap her, throw her out of my house? I looked at her, I mean, I turned toward the place her voice was coming from (as for seeing, really seeing, you couldn't see anything there) and I responded in kind: "Do you know that Chelo Velázquez wrote that bolero when he was seventeen years old?" We were even. She laughed out loud, I swear to you it was the miserable laugh of a damned rodent. "Fleas," she said, "wait for their hosts to fornicate before they fornicate too. In this way they can use the rabbit's nest to make their own nests." I asked her how the flea could know that the rabbit was fornicating. "By the ears," she replied, "their ears get hot during coitus." Angela, why aren't we in the Caribbean now, you and I, passionate and free, on a solitary island where your husband's tantrums can't reach us, or the foreigner's disgusting stories, or the melancholy longing of any bolero, this bolero. A desert island where I can have you all the time, without waiting for a divine power—that other rabbit—to decide when and how we can copulate. Think about this, think that perhaps tomorrow I'll be far away, very far from you.

Abel

Somos

We Are

On the Rue de la Marine, across from the docks of Grand Bourg—the liveliest place on Marie Galante—is the Club Raïssa. You can either sit outside, looking at the ocean and the packet boats going back and forth to Pointe-à-Pitre, or settle inside, in the dim light of the cheap café that smells of wet tobacco. Julieta and I stayed inside, ordered a bottle of Elixir de la Marie Galante, and drank it in silence. Celia hadn't come with us—on the previous day she had discovered a solitary island across from the town of Gosier, decided she wanted to go there, climbed aboard a fishing boat, and with the exhausting trip and the fatigue of spending time on the beach and being out in the sun, she was worn out. It was almost dark when she returned to the ship. I reproached her for being late—we're too old, she and I both, for that kind of running around. She looked pale and had scratches on her arms. She said she would eat in the cabin but if I wanted to I could go up to the dining room. I agreed immediately—it was the only chance I would have to eat supper alone with Julieta. Celia smiled, a strange smile on that haggard face. She fell into bed and I asked her, for the first time in more than twenty years, to please not go to sleep without taking a shower. She laughed and I insisted: "You smell like a monkey." She laughed again. I would have sworn she'd had too much to drink: "I smell like roses, Fernando, nothing but roses." I thought suddenly of Bermúdez—I hadn't been thinking about anybody, not even Elena, everyone seemed so distant—and then suddenly Bermúdez: women on ships lose their inhibitions. And there was Celia, a good mother, a good wife, an excellent homemaker, transformed by this cruise into a perfect lunatic. When I was at the door I asked if she needed anything. She said yes, would I turn off the light. An inhuman stink was floating in the cabin, and I hesitated. "If I turn it off," I said, "you'll fall asleep without showering." I left and looked for Julieta. We chose an out-of-the-way table, and she didn't even ask for Celia, she was happy that we were alone. I was happy too, I had a lot of things to say to her, I wanted to tell her, for example, that it had all started on the night we visited San Juan, did she remember I had gotten sick? She nodded and took my hand, how could I forget, then I confessed that the emotion I felt watching her eat sushi had excited me so much I had ejaculated a cappella, you might say, not caring about anything, like an adolescent. Even worse, I added, because in my adolescence I never lost control like that. A thing like that happening to me at this stage of my life, after Elena's wedding, when I had no plans except to take it easy with Celia, a quiet cruise, no great excitement—except maybe the dead man this morning—a thing like that happening to me almost at the end. A mournful silence fell, which she broke by saying it had taken her by surprise too, between giving harp lessons and taking care of her mother—it was the first time she had mentioned her mother—her life was well organized, she had a set routine that showed no signs of changing. True, she still mourned her trumpeter, for a long time she had wanted to go on a cruise that would bring her to Marie Galante, it took her years to save enough money and years to decide to do it. "But at last you're here," I said, in part to change the subject. The memory of that man irritated me—I envied the mystery of his death, nobody traveled so far to die like that, falling into the maw of the Great Abyss, nobody who wasn't a little crazy. "They ruled it a suicide," Julieta declared, "but I know it wasn't. He wasn't that kind of man." The phrase amused me, "that kind of man," and tears filled her eyes. "It had to be an accident," she kept on. "I've always said it was an accident." And that was enough, of course, her word against nobody's. "It happens sometimes," I said, supporting her. "You'd be amazed if I told you the number of tourists who die every year far from home, I read it the other day in *Travel & Leisure*." She was lost in thought, I didn't think she even heard me, but she raised her hand to stop me: "Agustín Conejo was no tourist, he was working, they hired him and the orchestra on a cruise ship." I wondered if I had heard correctly: what did she say his name was? She repeated it: Agustín Conejo.

Agustín Rabbit. I thought with a name like that there weren't many things you could be in life, perhaps least of all a harpist. Confessions faded away and we concentrated on the meal. We both had a good appetite but were also hungry for other things, hungry to devour each other, digest and regurgitate each other, especially regurgitate. To excite me she ran the tip of her tongue around the rim of the glasses, touched me with her foot, forced me to tell her again the cruel story of the *dugongs*, those buxom creatures martyrized along the coast of Mombasa; the ignoble story of the sows driven wild by their boars' saliva; the edifying story of the hyenas, endowed by nature with a long, formidable clitoris capable of provoking orgasms from beyond the grave. It was almost midnight when we said good night. I left her at her cabin and went to mine, and as soon as I opened the door I was overwhelmed by the same burning stink that had been there when I left. Celia, predictably enough, had fallen asleep with the light on and, naturally, had not taken a shower. I walked to the bed very quietly and watched her for a while. I felt a mixture of tenderness and concern: it was her familiar flesh giving off an unfamiliar smell. Later I heard her snore, it was cruel, we're very cruel, that was when I left the cabin and decided to spend the night with Julieta.

When I came back the next morning, Celia was dressed and waiting for me. She assumed I had gone out very early, "at the crack of dawn," she said, without a shred of irony, then asked that we have breakfast together, and during breakfast she mentioned that she didn't plan to get off at Marie Galante. It occurred to me it might be a trick. I observed her warily as she told me about her demented excursion to that dream island, I understood, she concluded, she was exhausted. Her reasoning seemed normal to me.

Julieta and I did get off. Grand Bourg, at that hour, was a miniature hell, everything cooking in the same pot, everything glinting, everything almost burning. She clung to my arm and said she had to get to the place right away—she was referring to the Abyss—remember she had to keep a promise. I went out to find a taxi and came back with the driver, a corpulent black with drooping eyelids who insisted I tell him how long we were planning to stay there. I guessed a couple of hours, in reality I didn't know. We agreed on the fare and started out. It was a short, hot, miserable trip, the car bouncing from side to side on a dreadful road overgrown with vines. We had to stop, not long after we left Grand Bourg, so that Julieta could get out and vomit. I felt nauseated too. It was the driver, he gave off a smell very similar to the one Celia had brought back the night before, and only hot air came in the windows. It was hard, terribly hard, getting to the Great Abyss. How did a trumpet player ever end up dying in such a desolate hole? The taxi finally stopped at the foot of a hill; the driver looked at us: now we'd have to climb up. And we climbed up. I covered my head with my handkerchief that was soaked with perspiration and took Julieta by the hand. The man, much more agile than we were, quickly reached the top. "Apa-li!" he shouted in Creole, "la gueule Grand Gouffre!" Julieta couldn't catch her breath; I believe she tried to say something but fainted instead.

When she came to, Julieta burst into tears. She pleaded not to go yet and held on to my arm; she was still very weak.

We must have been a peculiar sight because the driver didn't stop looking at us, an incredulous look, even a little sly. Julieta managed to get to her feet, and I put my arm around her waist and led her to the protective railing at the precipice, two crossed timbers that creaked in the gusting wind. We looked down, the whirlpools at the bottom, a pit of vertigo, my body pressed against the back of her body that smelled of vomit and smelled of sweat. A strange odor of sex seemed to come from under her clothes, a sour aroma that intoxicated me, I felt repelled and giddy, I wanted to get to it, to the source of that odor, absorb it completely with my nose and tongue. "Let's go," I said. I thought she would faint again, she was leaning heavily against me, gasping, almost as if she were in a trance. I kissed her neck, I licked the sweaty, acid nape of her neck. "Not here," she moaned. "Not here." I pulled her to the car and signaled to the driver that we were leaving. She lay down in the backseat and I unbuttoned her blouse. The car pulled away and the torture began again; in half an hour, I thought, it will all be over. I patted her lightly on the cheeks, I fanned her with a piece of cardboard and raised her skirt a little: that stench hit me all at once—she wasn't wearing underwear. I caressed her thighs, I scratched at her pubis, I risked my middle finger, a solitary finger that snaked around her pubic hair, she moaned softly and barely moved. I opened her blouse a little more and her nipples appeared, two large purplish circles with pupils that looked in another direction. She took my hand and placed it between her legs, then the intensity of her moans increased, she was flailing around like a madwoman. The driver slowed down and gave us a sideways glance. Julieta was sucking a finger, rubbing her belly, pinching her buttocks. The man slammed on the brakes and turned around. I held his gaze for just an instant, and then I raised Julieta's skirt, his eyes moved to her gray, wet, wide-open sex, she rubbed herself with my hand, she arched in the seat, she put out her tongue, a thick tongue looking for the way. I opened the door and got out of the car, and then I opened the driver's door. He looked me up and down, hesitated for a moment, and got out too. I moved back, staggering, and he undressed in front of me, I saw his dark skin, darker than black, much darker, almost blue, I saw him from the front, I looked quickly at his savage tool, a real instrument for causing pain, I saw him get in the back door and had what *National Geographic*—or is it *Psychology Today*? —calls a flashback. I thought of Elena, my daughter Elena getting in the backseat of her boyfriend's car late at night, and a lump came to my throat. I moved closer without making noise and looked in the window. I could hardly see Julieta, he was covering her with his body, but I did hear her panting, grunting, whispering half-finished phrases that went with her tongue into the depths of that black ear. The heat intensified by the second, it was as if a ball of fire, of steam, of death had descended. The scene drove me out of my mind, shattered me in a matter of seconds. I opened my mouth and a thread of saliva dribbled out, I stroked myself, I concentrated on the driver's back, fascinated by the hard labor of his buttocks, two sets of perfect muscles that rose and fell, when they fell Julieta moaned again, then he consoled her, whispered words I couldn't understand, looked for her lips, gave her interminable kisses, wet, noisy, there was a sharp noise when their sexes met and another when they parted. At last she gave a final howl—or was it my howl?—was rigid for as long as the shout lasted, and then went limp, turned into a rag. He continued to make love to her, perhaps more violently, and in a thin hoarse voice she asked him to let her be, her body couldn't take any more, she couldn't stand any more. The man sat up, I thought for a moment he was going to get out of the car, but instead of that he moved over Julieta, lifted himself to her face, and brought his sex to her lips. It was all very fast, he roared five or six times and collapsed, frothing at the mouth, moaning softly, sounding like a woman. In a little while he moved away and then he did get out of the car, picked up his clothes, and looked at me coldly while he dressed. I went in to see Julieta, she was still lying on the seat, her face covered with the spiderweb of the driver's sperm. I took out my handkerchief and began to wipe it away. She opened her eyes, they were still absent, I helped her to sit up, I buttoned her blouse myself, I smoothed her hair with my fingers. The man got behind the wheel again but didn't look at us for the rest of the trip. When we reached Grand Bourg he limited himself to asking where he should drop us. I remembered the Club Raïssa and asked him to take us there. When we got out he turned and sat looking at Julieta. She stopped too, they exchanged glances, they had enjoyed it, I thought, everything they did they had enjoyed. Julieta sighed. There were dark circles under her eyes. I asked her where she wanted to sit, and she asked that we go inside, she'd had enough sun. We ordered the bottle of Elixir de la Marie Galante, and in the dim light of the café the green liquor luminesced like a damn lamp. I took her hand and she pulled it back, stared at me, spoke in a voice unlike her own: I was a pig, she said, and she never wanted to see me again. I ordered another bottle—there was still some left in the one we were drinking, but I ordered another one—I poured her a glass, put it in her hands, and kissed her on the mouth, the mouth that was tired of so much kissing. Her face was sticky, I told her so, I asked her if she knew what was on her cheeks, I licked her eyelids, she'd go on seeing me even if she didn't want to, we still had a lot to do, I had seen her taking her pleasure with a man, now I had to see her making love to a woman. She said pig, she said it three or four times, and I slapped her. She responded by throwing the liquor in my face, I told her I'd kill her, but first I wanted to see her doing it with a woman, a black girl with hard breasts, smooth belly, agile thighs, a hot black girl bathed in sweat, that smell got me excited, sweaty bodies drove me wild, we'd go find her, they'd both have to do what I said, kiss each other's lips, lick each other's bellies, pull out each other's pubic hairs one by one, and remember, I'd be right there, if I ordered her to go down she'd have to go down, put the tip of her tongue between those wet buttocks, suck the flesh of that crotch, Julieta, let herself be masturbated by the black girl's nipple, hard nipples, when they rubbed against her clitoris they'd set her on fire, see what a good time she'd have, trust me, she'd enjoy it, hadn't she enjoyed it with the driver?

tell me, sow (I grabbed her by the hair), did she enjoy it or not? she said yes, a very faint yes, louder, I shouted, let me hear it, tell me if you enjoyed it, tell me if you felt it, if it wasn't a fact that nothing in this world had hurt as much as that man's cock, did it hurt or not? she said yes, louder, bitch, and she shouted yes, yes, yes it did . . .

Angela:

your emissary—our emissary—sometimes comes to the house and eats cookies while I finish writing to you. Yesterday, for the first time, he saw the sketches the foreigner draws, for the most part they show animals fornicating, details of their sexual organs, very explicit pictures I'm not sure a boy of his age should see. He looked at the drawings for a long time, and when the foreigner came in he asked her a good number of questions about them. Today he's back, right now he's sitting beside her, and she, by the way, is very patient with him, we must acknowledge what is true. A moment ago he came in for his cookies and I gave him this letter for you, but he said he wasn't leaving yet, he was with Mickey—he calls her Mickey—and he told me some of what he had learned, and believe me, it's quite a lot. I suggested he not tell anyone that Mickey was teaching him those things, in any event he should say he had read about them. "Where?" he asked. "Say that you read them in National Geographic,*" and I showed him a copy of the magazine, the American magazine that the foreigner receives with so much enthusiasm. Even now, as I write these lines to you, I hear him asking how slugs kiss (I suppose they must be eternal, wet, deep kisses), because even slugs, Angela, are kissing behind our backs.*

Abel

Without opening my eyes I heard the hum of the silence. I listened for a while to see if I could make out some other sound. Then I slowly raised my eyelids and saw the silhouette of Celia sitting on the edge of the bed. I hesitated about letting her know I was awake; the last memory that floated by was the Club Raïssa, Julieta's maddened eyes, the venomous green of the Elixir de la Marie Galante. Other, more recent things were fragments of dreams. I had dreamed a good deal, who knows for how many hours, dreams that were terribly dark and real.

"Sleeping Beauty returns to earth. How do you feel after your heart attack?"

Sarcasm was not her forte, it never had been, but one thing was clear: Celia was prepared for war. After so many years of seeing each other asleep and awake, there was no point in trying to deceive her. It wasn't even necessary to talk, she knew by instinct: now he's asleep, now he's on the border, now he's awake. It's depressing to know there are no surprises, and a relief to know there aren't any. I asked her where we were. She stood and turned on the light. We were on a ship, darling, didn't I even remember that? I sat up, tried to orient myself, tie up loose ends. I had no idea how I'd gotten to the cabin, I didn't even remember taking off my clothes. But here I was, naked, stark naked, my whole body throbbing with pain.

"I know very well I'm on a ship," I said. "I wanted to know if we've left Marie Galante."

"You and I have," Celia answered. "We're on our way to Martinique."

I drank three glasses of water, one after the other, stumbled to the bathroom, and pissed a burning, thick urine that looked greenish to me. I went back to bed. Celia seemed very tense, I still hadn't answered her question: how did I feel after the heart attack? I didn't like the tone of her voice, and I didn't like the way she kept pestering me. I didn't like this woman at all, this perfect stranger.

"You were dreaming," she said. "You clawed at your chest and shouted. I was frightened and called the doctor again. He told me not to worry, you were just drunk."

I tried to remember. I knew I had dreamed about her, about Angela the Beauty, a flesh-and-blood dream where I heard her singing. I heard her singing, but I really knew she was crying. In dreams you see one thing and it's something else, you see a strange face and you know it's your mother, for example. It's the only part of life where you can act on what you feel, not what you see.

"I thought you were dreaming about your heart attack. Don't you have any little shooting pains?"

Celia wanted to fight, it was normal. And I had no desire for a quarrel, which was also normal. "It takes two to tango," I thought, and one was missing, my part was missing, the part of my life that wanted no more fighting. I lit a cigarette and confessed that I didn't feel good or bad, for the moment I was sunk in a kind of spiritual and physical limbo, I had lost my fear of a heart attack, I wasn't afraid anymore of dying of a myocardial infarction, just see how much good the trip had done me. She smiled, malevolent and calculating. Good, she said, she was very happy about that, one less bit of hypochondria in my life, but in any case I must have dreamed something horrible to shout like that, try to remember, it's a good idea to tell your nightmares so they won't come true.

"It was no nightmare. I dreamed about Angela the Beauty."

"Ahhhh," Celia exclaimed, "your granny, the dyke."

It was a low blow, too mean-spirited an attack. Celia and I had spent the best moments of our engagement with Angela. In her house we could hear our fill of boleros—toward the end the poor woman only wanted to hear that music, the same songs that had seasoned her romance with Marina, because in her later years Angela fell desperately in love with another woman, a passion that reached its height when I was still a child. That was precisely what my dream was about. I had come to her house in the suburbs—Angela always lived in the suburbs and I always dreamed about her house—bringing her a letter from her lover (it was my job to carry the letters), and she took me into the music room, turned on the phonograph, and played the latest record of Leo Marini. That's where the dream ended. In real life, the ritual was much longer and more complicated. Angela would touch the letter and not open it, put on another record, usually Pedro Vargas. "I'd like to be the charms of your beautiful eyes, the love magic of your arms." She would kiss the envelope, open it with utmost care, take out the paper, and I would watch her eyes, the expression that would change as she read: she would smile, shake her head, laugh out loud. Then she would put it away, she would put it in her pocket and give me a radiant look; that bolero, she said, listen to it carefully, and she would begin to sing, she had a husky voice, strong, somewhat mannish, she would sing and act out the song. I thought it was very funny, I would double over laughing, throw myself on the floor to giggle, then my grandfather would appear, always in a bad mood, look at the two of us, let's see if we could cut out the racket, then he would disappear, we would see his silhouette fading behind the glass door, and my grandmother would make a face, take out the envelope, and kiss it again.

"It's good you dreamed about her," said Celia. "She's probably calling you."

They called her Angela the Beauty because she really had been beautiful. When I knew her she was already a mature woman, she must have been about the same age I am now, I don't know, maybe a little older. Her hair was white, how curious, she'd had white hair since she was young, like Julieta. I must have been eight years old at the time, nine at most. Marina would visit us in the afternoons, she'd bring a book of poems and they would sit on the small sofa in the living room, Marina reading and Angela embroidering, and after a while my grandmother would complain of a pain in her back and rest her head on her friend's skirt, and the other woman would caress her forehead, smooth her hair, lean over to kiss her nose, a brief kiss, too brief, but one that always filled me—I watched everything from the floor—with great happiness. After a while, if my grandfather was out of the house, the two women would get up and go to the music room. My grandmother would put on a record, "I loved once, only once, in my life," and when I tried to follow she would lock the door and shout at me from inside the room to leave them alone. I'd put my ear to the door, try to look through the cracks, but I never could see or hear anything. When the music ended, "fiesta bells sing in my heart," a great silence fell, that was all. The next day, on my way home from school, I would pass by Marina's house, she'd be waiting for me with a letter in her hands, give this to your granny, she would say, and kiss me on the nose. If she hadn't finished writing it yet, she'd give me something to eat, and I would enjoy chewing on chicken bones—something I wasn't allowed to do at home—and watch as she found her inspiration. Marina talked to herself, smiled, shook her head, laughed out loud, and allowed her eyes to fill with tears. Then she would kiss the paper before placing it in the envelope.

"Your granny was pretty shameless too," Celia added. "You didn't fall too far from the tree, you know."

Many years later, Celia and I made it our habit to visit Angela the Beauty, who by then was quite frail and almost blind. They were musical evenings that would last until ten, sometimes as late as midnight. My grandmother insisted on Celia's reading Marina's old letters, on reading them aloud so she could hear them again. Celia would use a cold, distant voice that never, ever moved us. By that time Marina was gone, she had died five or six years earlier, but for my grandmother she had died long before, when she fell in love with another woman, a foreigner who looked like a mouse and wouldn't allow her to visit us. Then I would come home from school without bringing anything, not a note, not a word of farewell, not a brief kiss of remembrance. The world fell in on Angela the Beauty, and she would ask me to play the Leo Marini record, "but what does life matter if we are apart," and would cry, staining the upholstery on the sofa with tears and mucus. My grandfather would pass by, always in a bad mood, look at us without saying a word, and his figure would slowly fade behind the glass door. Marina used to sign her letters with the pseudonym Abel, so that at first Celia thought the letters she was reading to my grandmother came from an old boyfriend, a very passionate old man who, she told me later, could think of nothing but eating the Beauty's voluptuous body raw. It wasn't until my grandmother died—Elena had just been born—that I could tell her the truth: Abel was Marina, Angela the Beauty was her lover, Mickey (because she looked like a mouse) was the name she gave the foreigner who had come between them.

"'We Are,'" Celia recalled, "was your grandmother's song. In her old age she turned to that."

She died listening to it; my mother told me she had to play it for her seventeen times before Angela lapsed into a coma. The priest came and ordered her to turn off the phonograph, and Angela the Beauty, offended and trembling, ordered her to play it again. Then she made her confession, she accused herself out loud of having loved another woman, of having felt indescribable pleasure sucking her breasts, of going mad with passion when she rubbed this sex, Father, this sinful clam that the worms will eat tomorrow, against the adored cunt of a faithless woman who eventually left her for another. The priest tried to make her be quiet, he offered hurried forgiveness and left her to her fate, lulled to sleep by the singing of Leo Marini: "we are nothing more than that . . . nothing more."

"But you, old age is turning you to other things."

Celia was on the attack again, desperately trying to wound me, and I felt sorry for her. My head was burning, my eyes were burning, but I had an appetite. I asked her what time it was, and she said it was two in the morning. I started up in bed. It wasn't possible, how long had I slept?

"I have no idea," she said. "I didn't bother to keep track. But if you like, we can do it now. You fell asleep, or I should say, you were thrown unconscious into that bed at about three in the afternoon. You've been sleeping off your hangover for exactly eleven hours."

Now I remembered everything, or almost everything. On the walls in the restaurant where Julieta and I drank the Elixir, there were photographs of Raisa Gorbachev, dozens of photographs, Mrs. Gorbachev ruled over the Rue de la Marine, across from the docks of Grand Bourg, which is the liveliest place on Marie Galante. It occurred to me that this dive was a front, I gave a speech attacking traffickers and pirates (there was never a lack of pirates on Marie Galante), I stood up and shouted obscenities, I tore one of the photographs off the wall, ripped it into a thousand pieces in front of Julieta's desolate eyes. The man who was waiting on us vanished and reappeared a little later, accompanied by a large man in a turban, some kind of Hindu, who was irritated and boorish and ordered us to leave the table. I know I tried to reach out for Julieta, I know I tried to tell her we were leaving, that's all I know. When I came to, I heard the hum of silence, the natural hum of the cabin, and I lay there with my eyes closed, waiting for a miracle.

"They must have drugged us. I'm sure they gave us poison."

Celia threw her head back, showed her teeth, but made no sound.

"I can understand their giving you poison"—even her voice had changed—"that's what you give to rats, isn't it?"

I regretted it deeply but I had to ask about Julieta, I had to find out some basic facts—how we had gotten out of the Club Raïssa, how we had gotten back to the ship. I took a deep breath, as if I were going under water, and asked her to tell me everything. She smiled in triumph. That was exactly what she had been waiting for, that was the only reason she had spent so many hours at my side, watching over me in the dark, gauging my breathing.

"Two blacks brought you. Julieta stayed behind."

I shook my head, I looked at her helplessly, I had no more air left and I was at the bottom, at the fucking bottom of the abyss, she ought to take pity on me, at least tell me the rest.

"She came back to the ship too, they brought her with you, except she was still on her feet—not you, you were like a dead man—and she got her things and said she was staying on Marie Galante. Forever."

I closed my eyes and thought of Angela the Beauty. I thought of her because I wanted to, I had to rescue her melody, just one song in that sugary sea of boleros. Then I realized that every good dream has its hidden rules, its sharp thorn, its dark side. "I brought you a letter," I said to my grandmother, to the face of my grandmother and the voice of my grandmother, but hidden beneath were the face and gestures of Julieta. Julieta the Beauty. Not ever again.

Joséphine Beauharnais ruled over the Black Angus. The Black Angus was in Fort-de-France. And we were in Fort-de-France. It was that simple. I was dressed in white, trousers, shoes, polo shirt, all the same color, and a Panama hat that Celia bought for me as soon as we walked off the ship. The bar was very similar to the Club Raïssa, a cheap café, damp and deserted at that time of day, differing from the club on Marie Galante in only one thing: it was well lit, the light came in through the skylights in the ceiling and you felt yourself floating in a silent, tragic atmosphere, as if you were floating in a place of death. A crude illustration, stained with mildew, reigned over the place: the Empress Joséphine, born on Martinique, having love made to her by an island black, the slave's cock, like a purple anaconda, curling around her body, the head of the animal between her breasts, the cruel tongue deep in her nipple. At first Celia thought it was Cleopatra. Then she got up, moved as close to it as she could, and yielded to the evidence: "Joséfine, enfin tu es mienne," said the inscription.

She stood there, looking at the picture, motionless, and it occurred to me that she wasn't really looking at it. Finally she came back to the table with a few questions. At this stage of the game, she said, it made no sense for us to separate, it didn't even make sense to lie. She looked into my eyes. Tell the truth, Fernando, how many times had I gone to bed with Julieta. I said three, maybe four. She lowered her eyes. She had read somewhere that all harpists were a little sluttish, maybe it was the position, you know, their legs always spread wide, with the harp right there. I was suffocating, I felt impotent, old, stupid. Celia asked where we had done it. I was a canary, a poor stool pigeon, I didn't tell for the sake of telling, I confessed so I wouldn't forget, she would be my memory. We had done it everywhere, in her cabin, that was Lisbon 16, on a staircase in Pointe-à-Pitre, even in the water. It was nice to do it in the ocean, your bodies float, women's breasts stay on the surface, half in, half out of the water, but cocks have to struggle against the vulgar schizophrenia in temperatures, hot inside, cold in the ocean. Celia listened very seriously, very attentively, as if I were talking about a profound subject. There was no way to know what she was feeling. I told her Julieta's pubis was gray, almost white, actually, it was like the pubis of an old lady, like violating your own grandmother. She smiled, opened her purse, and took out an envelope: "She had the nerve to leave this letter for you." She extended her arm and I didn't move a muscle, didn't show any sign of touching that paper. She dropped it on the table and I broke into a cold sweat, I fanned myself with my hat. "Read it," she said. "You can read it if you want." I understood I had two choices: the first, to tear it up; the second, more dramatic one, to give it back to her so she could read it herself; the story was over. It was a masterstroke. Celia picked up the letter, opened the envelope, and I stood up, excused myself, said I was going to look at the illustration: "Joséfine, enfin tu es mienne," the climbing cock imprisoning breasts, thighs, and hips. I wanted Joséphine, I wanted Julieta, I felt an irresistible desire to embrace her, chew her sinful flesh, sink my teeth into her blind nipples. It was the last time I was going to feel a passion like this, and I ought to say good-bye with my eyes on the infinite, I knew I was leaving something or someone, perhaps myself, in this ruinous bar on Martinique, this squalid, empty dive, this asshole of the world. I turned and went back to the table. Celia was holding the letter in the envelope. She held it and then she tore it into a thousand pieces that fell to the floor. "She wasn't a harpist," she said. I held my breath, I prepared myself for the worst, but she didn't say anything else. We paid, and then we left the Black Angus. In Fort-de-France we saw people boarding up windows; somebody said a hurricane was coming. I thought of Bermúdez, he had warned me about that too; from June to November the Caribbean was a devil. Celia was excited—maybe the ship wouldn't sail—and I was terrified. All I wanted now was to leave, not see all those people, forget I had ever set foot on Marie Galante, wipe away everything, everything, everything . . . a hurricane could wipe it all away.

The ship did sail, much to the sorrow of Celia, who missed her chance to see a hurricane. That night we ate on board; Julieta's shadow fluttered a few times between us. We both thought about her, almost at the same time I'm sure, and we both avoided mentioning her. We did talk about Elena. Little by little we were returning to normality, to everyday topics. I regretted not having bought her a present. Celia smiled, she had thought of everything, she had bought her a pin on Guadeloupe, in that place called Gosier, Gosier, Gosier—she repeated it as if it were a magic spell, the abracadabra that opened I don't know which doors in her mind. She was lost in thought, and another shadow, I couldn't tell exactly whose, also flew over our heads. Otherwise we had a quiet supper, ate dessert, and finally went out to stroll on the deck. The night was cool, it was the first cool night after so many days of blistering heat. Celia took my hand and I had the feeling she was going to say something horrible: "The trumpet player didn't die in any abyss." Now more than ever I had to show my self-restraint. I stood motionless and saw a kind of reddish light on the horizon, the reflection of one of the islands we were leaving behind. It brought a lump to my throat. "He lives with her, they married ten years ago." These were the confessions in the letter, the words that had been torn to pieces, mixed with the sawdust on the floor of the Black Angus. "Ah, and her name isn't Julieta." I controlled my astonishment, I acted like a man, I even smiled. It was getting to be time for us to go back to the cabin. I put my arm around her shoulders, and we began to walk. I thought it wouldn't be prudent to be completely silent, I was prepared to make a final comment, something trivial, it was perhaps the last time I would speak to her about it, so I told her, I told her that Julieta, or whatever her name was, had a good imagination for that kind of thing, I mean, for inventing names. "Do you know what she said the trumpet player's name was?" We stopped in front of the door and I took out the key. Celia shivered almost imperceptibly; perhaps she had the feeling that now I would be the one who was going to say something terrible. "No," she said, "she didn't mention it in her letter." I paused. We went into the cabin, and I poured her a drink. "Sit down, and I'll tell you."

La última noche que pasé contigo

The Last Night I Spent with You

▟ ▲ ▙

Angela:

this morning, even before I got up, I turned on the radio. I was alone in my bed (no matter what you think, that woman, that foreigner, as you call her, isn't sleeping with me yet), I was alone and they began to play our song. I turned up the volume, I pulled the covers over my head, I thought, it's a shame we've never spent the night together, it's a shame because a lover never knows how vulnerable and gentle the other one is until he sees him sleeping. We never saw each other sleeping, do you understand, Angela? That's the great lack in our affair. When the bolero was finished, I was crying, imagining how it would have been to spend a night with you, transplanting the experiences of all those afternoons we spent together into the densely packed heart of the night we've never had. A little later I pulled down the covers and saw that Julieta (the foreigner is named Julieta, now it's time for us to call her by name) was standing at the door, she was crying too, watching me suffer on your account. She had just gotten up, her hair was disheveled and she was wearing a transparent robe, perhaps blue, perhaps yellow, I imagined she was cold, in reality she was trembling, and so I moved to one side, lifted the quilt, and asked her to come to bed. She agreed, she curled up beside me, and little by little we began to warm up. She is much younger than we are, but probably much wiser. Her face is ugly, you know that, but she has a splendid body and it suddenly occurred to me that the three of us could have been very happy together. We spent the morning in bed, got up late, she prepared breakfast, and when your grandson came to see me I had not written a single line. The poor thing stopped at the door, "There's no letter today," I told him, his expression broke my heart and he said he could wait, he would wait as he had other times until I finished writing it. I glanced into Julieta's eyes, she looked at me so severely it frightened me, this girl is very wise, "There's no letter," I repeated to your grandson, and looked at her again, she was watching me with that menacing expression. When the boy left she came up behind me, put her arms around me, and took me to her lair, the room that holds all her secrets and intimate smells, she pushed me down on the bed and there we stayed until it grew dark. It was marvelous, this woman is very skilled, no one would think she could be so strong and so delicate at the same time, an oriental sensibility for love, she is meticulous, tenacious, a perfectionist. . . . She said we would go on sleeping in separate rooms, she decided it knowing I will obey her, at least for the first few months. Later, later I'll stay in her room or she'll come to sleep in mine, because I want to see her sleeping, I want to hear the noises she makes when she's chewing on some horrible nightmare, I want to know her nocturnal miseries, the way her hair tangles, the way her mouth opens and stays open, the gases and smells that come out of her naked body, I don't need to tell you that we'll sleep naked.

I found out this morning, don't ask me how, that this relationship with the foreigner will be definitive. That doesn't mean I'll die at her side, or that I'll die for her sake, but I will die with her taste on my lips. When she leaves, if she ever does one day, I'll say good-bye with my eyes on the infinite, certain that I too am leaving something. I think you probably don't understand me, I probably will never send you this letter, I probably won't even say good-bye to you. One of the things that will make me sad is not seeing Fernando again, that boy has made me think. This morning, for example, I was looking into his eyes and I pitied his innocence, his frustration at not being able to bring you a letter, and then I wondered what loves, what ecstasies, what sorrows will shake him when he is an adult. I'd like to think that he too, at the end of his life, will try to consume his fears in the impossible vertigo of late passion, that he will know how to treasure those moments, that the memory of a redeeming afternoon, the brilliant memory of an afternoon of love, will become in his mind the memory of a last night of passionate love, the night he may not have spent with anyone, the same one I never, ever spent with you . . .